Bright Sun,
Dark Moon

Also by Frances Patton Statham

Flame of New Orleans

Jasmine Moon

Daughters of the Summer Storm

Phoenix Rising

From Love's Ashes

On Wings of Fire

To Face the Sun

Mary Musgrove, Queen of Savannah
(Original Title: Call the River Home)

Trail of Tears

The Roswell Women

The Roswell Legacy

The Silk Train

Mountain Legacy

Murder, al fresco

Bright Sun, Dark Moon

Frances Patton Statham

Bocage Books

ISBN: 978-0-9895007-0-8

(Previously ISBN: 441 08040)

First Edition: September 1975 by Ace Books
Second Edition: November 2013 by Bocage Books

Library of Congress Control Number: 2013917670

bocagebooks@mindspring.com
www.bocagebooks.com

Cover design by Steve McAfee

10 9 8 7 6 5 4 3 2

To

Meredith and Kathleen

"And who is she that looketh forth in the morning,
fair as the moon, bright as the sun, and terrible as an
army with banners?"

Song of Solomon 6:10

Bright Sun,
Dark Moon

Chapter 1

Charleston—February 2, 1803

*I*n an old deserted mansion on the banks of the Ashley River, Sonia Beauveau sat in the once elegant drawing room, where time seemed to stand still. Silence hung like the limp damask draperies dusted with a patina of neglect.

The woman had been lost in her own thoughts, but now her attention returned to the small, determined face before her.

In repose, the girl resembled a cold and un-attainable Renaissance beauty captured on some Italian canvas of a bygone age. The double-fringed, golden lashes, easily seen at arm's length, tended to disappear at a distance, leaving only the fragile, mystical glance of a Botticelli or Da Vinci. Yet, when the amethyst eyes came alive, they announced her spirited heritage from the Carter family.

"And what makes you so sure you'll succeed?" the woman asked, breaking the silence. "Will you swoon at the man's feet and expect to be carried into his house?"

The awakening was swift; the girl's eyes became two shining mosaics—yellow glints of fire in an amethyst setting.

"Oh, thank you for such a marvelous idea, Sonia," the girl exclaimed, clasping her arms around the woman's shoulders. "Yes, I see now how it can be done… When I—"

Sonia held up her hand. "I certainly didn't mean to give you any ideas, love. Now, forget this foolishness and come to New Orleans with me, instead."

"I can't, Sonia. I must stay here in Carolina and prove my brother's murderer. The clues are almost certain to be in that hateful man's house. All I need is a little time to look. And I intend to get back what he stole from my brother."

"I still wish you'd leave it to the authorities. I don't think it proper for a sweet innocent like you to be anywhere near a man with that kind of reputation… much less under his roof."

"The authorities have done nothing about it."

The woman continued on as if the girl had not spoken. "…Why it was rumored that he even took a mistress on the Grand Tour with him and flaunted her all over Europe. Now everyone in Charleston knows he's bedding the daughter of his overseer. Heaven help him if his mother were still alive." She put her hand to her throat in dismay.

"Well, it's my own affair," the girl said stubbornly. "After all, I *am* eighteen and able to take care of myself. And if he already has someone sharing his bed," she added with a twinkle, "then I shall be safe from that indignity." Her expression sobered again. "But Sonia, I'll need one small favor. May I ride your mare tomorrow? She'll come home when I give her a slap on her rump, and then she can't be traced."

"You're far too headstrong, my dear. You always were." Sonia's glare softened. "But you know I can't refuse my own godchild."

With that settled the girl spent the rest of the day planning and replanning her strategy. Luckily, her riding instructor had taught her how to fall from a horse without getting hurt, but she could easily pretend. She knew it was a dangerous venture, but wasn't that why she had come back to the Low Country — to make sure that her brother's murderer was punished?

Now alone and hidden in the house for that one night, she did not dare to build a telltale fire as evening approached. Instead, she wrapped herself in the heavy down quilt and went to bed in the dark. But she was unable to sleep. Lightning flashed outside the window and thunder rumbled menacingly, while the storm without and her personal storm within merged and then subsided....

Chapter 2

By midafternoon, when the February wind—the only remnant of the night's thunderstorm—was still strong, the young girl walked quickly across the secluded yard to the old stable and called to the sole occupant of the stalls. "Come, Lady—pretty Lady—I have a carrot for you..."

A few minutes later, anxious to be near the crossroads at the time that Garth Stevens rode home from the Exchange, she flew down the sandy road.

She was sorry to be wearing her elegant wine-colored riding habit; for it was the last present her brother had sent home to her.

She had placed it in her trunk; unworn, since Bart had not known that the horses had been sold and she had no need of it—until today.

A pity that it would probably be ruined, but it was necessary for the deception. It was imperative that she appear as a rich young gentlewoman; for who would allow a penniless orphan to remain overnight at Mosshaven, one of the wealthiest mansions along the river?

Her long pale gold hair, so easily streaked by the sun, was bound into a chignon and covered by the riding hat. She hated wearing a hat, but her mother had always insisted that no lady ever had gold hair streaked with silver. So out of deference to her mother's memory, she had once more covered her head.

The moss-hung trees went by one by one. When she had almost reached the crossroads, she slowed her mount to a walk, but the mare snorted her displeasure at being forced to stop in a clump of dogwood trees near the road.

She waited while a whippoorwill sang a staccato song in the dense thicket near her. In time, the song was answered at a distance. Scampering from his home in a rotten log, a chipmunk stopped and sniffed the air before going on his way.

And then there was only the sound of the wind in the trees.

Doubts began to swing back and forth on the incessant pendulum of the wind. What if, on this particular day, Garth Stevens didn't follow his usual schedule?

Or, seeing her horse as a runaway, he rescued her before she could fall? Or even worse, what if he didn't take her to Mosshaven, but to another house, not his own?

Her hands tightened on the reins as she re-membered the words her brother had written her, shortly before he was so brutally murdered….

"If anything happens to me, you can blame that blackguard, Garth Stevens. He has stolen something very valuable from me, but I intend to get it back...."

Lady's ears pricked up, and a split second later the girl heard the sound of hooves. Easy...easy—I must be within sight. The riding crop swept across the mare's flank and the nervous horse bolted from the clump of trees in angry surprise.

Faster—faster, she urged. Seeing the rider approaching, she knew she would need to make the accident look real. Not quite yet; let him get a little closer.

She rode the mare onward and making ready to fall, she lowered her boot out of its stirrup. The creaking noise above her caused her to look up in surprise, and the last thing she saw was the plunging limb from the old oak....

* * *

The flickering lights; the voices; the constant throbbing... Something had gone wrong. Why was this offending heaviness weighting her down, as if she were buried under a vast pile of rocks?

"Praise the Lawd! She's finally comin' around. A little thing like that didn't have much chance, tanglin' with a big ole tree limb."

She attempted to move, but another voice, deep and masculine, hurt her ears, while a strong hand pressed hers to her side. "No, you musn't move, cara mia."

She opened her eyes and then gasped at the hated

face staring at her…much too handsome…much too close. His searching look swept over her like a roaring, crashing wave, devastating her entire being— her hair, her eyes, her lips; even the hollow at the base of her throat. The onslaught was ruthless and she shuddered at his bold manner.

Seeing her tremble, he said, "Don't be afraid. You fell from your horse, and although you have a few bruises, I think you're going to be all right."

So now she had seen him—not from a distance, but up close, face to face— and far more dangerous. His stubborn jaw, his piercing blue eyes, and tremendous height made him appear an even worthier opponent than she had imagined.

But relieved that she had not been found out immediately, she sank back onto the sofa. Yet, her plans had not included the terrible headache that traveled along every nerve.

"Zellie, get another cold cloth," the man commanded. He stroked the long wild hair lying against her cheek.

The large black woman dipped a linen cloth into a basin of water, squeezed it out and handed it to the man kneeling beside the sofa.

As he placed the cold cloth on her forehead, she asked in a weak voice, "Who are you, sir?"

Still searching her face, he answered, "Garth Stevens." Then he explained, " I was riding home when I saw a falling limb knock you from your horse. Tell me where I can reach your family and I'll send word to them that you're safe."

She looked at him in bewilderment.

"Are you visiting friends?"

He waited while the amethyst eyes widened into a blank stare.

Frowning, he pursued his questioning. "What is your name?"

Still there was no answer, only a little moan that escaped her lips as her eyelids fluttered and closed.

"Do you not wish to reveal your name to me, or is it that you're hurt worse than I thought?"

In the following silence, he suddenly left the drawing room and the care of the young woman to Zellie, as he began to pace back and forth on the piazza.

Keeping her eyes closed, she listened to his agitated steps. What was he thinking? Was he trying to decide what to do with her?

Her own plans had seemed so simple. But now, she was unable to think coherently.

She seemed to be in a fog, unable to answer, unable to do anything but wait while she recovered her senses.

Chapter 3

*O*ut on the piazza, Garth Stevens was also trying to recover from the shock. In his house was the young woman who had plagued his dreams ever since he had seen her in the gardens at Middleton two years previously. When he had first caught a glimpse of her, it was as if he were remembering another life out of time. But before he could discover her name, or be introduced, she had vanished and any attempt to find her had met with complete failure.

So, in the frustration of trying to forget her, he had lived life to the fullest, but in the end, nothing had satisfied. And now, when he had almost succeeded in removing her from his thoughts, she had literally fallen at his feet.

He should have been pleased, but her sudden reappearance stirred up a massive resentment. Two wasted years of his life—and now the gods had decided to torture him again.

He had denied it at the time, but now he knew

that his obsession with her and his hope of finding her again had precipitated the purchase in Italy and France of those prohibitively expensive materials of lace, fine tulles, muslins and, worst of all, the gossamer white, embroidered silk suitable for a bride.

But as lethal as his resentment against her, he also acknowledged that he could not let her vanish from his life again. In the past he had always taken what he wanted, and the niceties of courtship were foreign to him. But she was destined to be his.

And this was Garth Stevens' dilemma.

A few minutes later, it was not that she actually heard someone come into the drawing room. Rather, it was the feeling that she was being stared at that caused her to open her eyes again.

"Who are you and where did you come from?" the hostile stranger asked.

The amber eyes staring at her were filled with animosity for her, and she was puzzled. Resenting the strident tone, she responded, "I...I could not tell you, even if I wished."

The tall, full-bosomed, earthy beauty responded, "So you think you can take him away from me. Well, I'll make sure you don't!" And she lifted her arm as if to strike her.

"Don't touch her, Maida!" Garth's massive frame was suddenly between them, protecting her from the threatened assault.

His defense angered her even further. "Why did you

bring her here, Garth?" Maida demanded.

"That's no concern of yours, Maida. And since you are here in my house uninvited, I suggest you leave immediately."

The unexpectedly harsh words hit home and Maida, changing her tone, said, "You were glad to see me the last time. And I was waiting for you today."

"It's over, Maida. I told you before…"

The anger reappeared in her eyes and her voice became bitter. "You can't do this to me, Garth Stevens. You'll be sorry you treated me this way. And I'll get even with this little trollop you brought home. Just wait and see."

Garth moved toward her. Maida hurriedly left the room, her steps echoing across the piazza, then disappearing in the soft sand of the yard.

Garth's attention returned to the girl lying on the sofa.

"I must apologize for that young woman's rudeness. She's my overseer's daughter, but her manners are lacking."

"She's very pretty."

"She's a common sunflower eclipsed by a rose." Suddenly, he smiled. "But since you haven't offered to give me your name, we'll have to find a suitable one for such a delicate flower as you, even if your petals are a bit bruised for the moment."

"You called me something earlier, did you not?"

"Yes. You reminded me of—" He shook his head, as if to erase a memory. "I called you cara mia, 'my dear one.' So Cara it's to be," he affirmed, "until you decide to tell me your own name. Is that agreeable?"

"One name is as good as another," she replied.

His gentle mood suddenly disappeared and he frowned at her. "And now since it's so late, unfortunately you'll be forced to stay the night."

What had caused such a rapid change? Did he suspect her? Or had her arrival ruined his plans for the evening?

"I'll carry you upstairs and Zellie can see to you. If you're hungry, one of the girls from the kitchen will bring you food."

"Please," she said, feeling his impatience. "I can walk."

But she was lifted into the air, in strong, crushing, uncompromising arms, and her throat constricted in fear. She was not so sure that she wanted to spend a night in the same house as her brother's murderer. But she had started this intrigue and must see it through.

"Zellie," he shouted. "Come and help this young lady."

He placed her unceremoniously on the bed and disappeared when Zellie came into the bedroom.

The black woman stared at the torn silk riding habit and shook her head. "Chile, how you gonna get home in those clothes?"

When she didn't respond, the woman continued, "But right now, we've got us another problem."

"Another problem?"

"Yes'm. If you gonna spend the night here, you got no bedtime clothes either. But I'll see what I can find."

Zellie left the room and a few minutes later, she returned with an oversized white nightgown, a relic from Garth's mother's trunk, the gown smelling vaguely of lavender.

"At least I found somethin' for you to sleep in tonight, but it's so big I wouldn't try to stand up in it if I was you. Apt to find it wrapped 'round your feet...."

The effort of removing the riding habit and slipping into the gown was too much for her in her weakened condition. And when the supper tray was brought, she had no appetite for the food.

"Jes' a little she crab soup, Miss Cara. You'll waste away if you don't eat."

But Cara could not be persuaded and finally, Zellie took the tray away.

When she was alone, Cara berated herself thoroughly. *Idiot! How did I manage to get under a limb just when it was falling? Now I can't get away tonight, even if I wanted to — and as for searching the house —*

Outside the sound of a horse galloping along the drive interrupted her thoughts. Was the display with Maida just for her benefit? And was Garth Stevens leaving to make amends with her? No wonder the man was upset with her sudden arrival. She had evidently kept him from his own little game.

Chapter 4

*I*n the upstairs bedroom, Cara's headache eased and she drifted into a fitful sleep. But in the middle of the night the familiar nightmare that lurked in the unswept corner of her mind returned in full force.

In the opposite bedroom, Garth was sleeping soundly, when a terrified scream from the other room awakened him, with the sound echoing throughout the house. He leaped from his bed, hurriedly lit a candle, and rushed across the hallway.

"Wake up, Cara," Garth said. "You're having a bad dream." He put down the flickering candle and lifted her out of the twisted bedcovers.

"Let me go. I can't reach him. Please...He's dying. Don't keep me from him," she begged. She struggled with the man, but he held her in his strong arms, his hand caressing the warm, velvet skin where the gown had fallen from her shoulders.

Cara's scream had also awakened Zellie. "Mister Garth, what you doin' in this chile's bedroom?" she demanded, pulling a robe around her ample frame.

"She evidently had demons chasing her in her sleep, And then she was tangled up in the bedclothes."

"Well, it ain't fitten for you to be here. Jes' get on to bed while I tend to 'er."

So Garth left, while Zellie remained until Cara was breathing normally again, with only an occasional moan. Then, she too went back to bed. A few hours later the darkness soon gave way to light.

The beauty of the room held no pleasure for her when she woke. The early morning sun, coming through the window, hurt her eyes, and she put up her hands to shield them.

Cara could still feel Garth's hand on her shoulder — as if the imprint were etched into her flesh. She was afraid of him; for she knew that in anger he was capable of murder, and she was here to prove it.

Her thoughts were interrupted by the sound of voices outside her door.

"Sorry, Mister Stevens. I couldn't get here any sooner. The boy brought your message to me last night, but you know how slow babies can be…."

There was a knock on the door and then Zellie called, "Miss Cara, the doctor's here to see you." And it was Zellie who walked in with him.

The fat, bald man was wheezing from his climb up the stairs, and his clothes, none too elegant, were wrinkled as if he had slept in them.

"Well, well, young lady, I hear you had a fall

from your horse, yesterday."

"Yes," the weak voice replied.

He observed that she was still shielding her eyes from the sun. "Eyes bothering you a bit this morning?"

He didn't wait for an answer, but removed her hand and peered at her closely. The smell of stale cigars and whiskey was on his breath. Finding the odor repugnant, Cara turned her head away from him.

"Looks like you have a concussion, little lady," he pronounced. "You'll soon be all right, though. Time usually heals.

"But you'll have to remain quiet for the next few days—no strenuous riding to hounds or dancing 'til the wee hours." He laughed and then asked, "Anything else bothering you?"

"I...I can't seem to remember who I am...."

He patted her arm in reassurance. "That won't last long. When word gets out, some young buck will come to claim you—eager to give you *his* name, even if you can't remember *yours.*"

He laughed again at his own wit and sailed out of the room, while Zellie watched him with a disapproving eye.

"Might as well ask a caterpillar to dance on his toes, as to get that man to be serious. Mister Garth shoulda sent to town for the white folk's doctor, instead of the plantation doctor," Zellie mumbled as she left the room.

A short time later, one of the girls from the kitchen brought a breakfast tray with far too much food— johnny cakes, grits, ham, and hot tea. But having eaten nothing the previous evening, Cara knew she needed to eat, so she forced herself to nibble at the food.

Once again Zellie entered the room. "I mended the ridin' habit as best I could, Miss Cara. But I wish there was somethin' else in the house that you could wear instead."

"It doesn't matter, Zellie. I'll be leaving soon. But thank you."

Cara pushed aside the breakfast tray and, with Zellie's help, she was soon dressed.

"She's ready, Mister Garth."

The man came into the bedroom, his riding boots heavy as he walked across the floor. Without even a "good morning," he reached down and picked her up in his arms.

"Where are you taking me?" Cara asked in a frightened voice.

"Downstairs, to the library." And then as if to soften his gruff manner, he added, "You can be the languishing beauty on the sofa there. Since we'll probably have visitors today, we have to think of your reputation. Zellie tells me it wouldn't do for a lady to have callers in her bedroom. And then there's a fire in the library to take away the morning chill."

They were halfway down the stairs when a knock sounded at the heavy front door.

"Just in time. That's probably the sheriff."

Cara stiffened in alarm. Sensing her reaction, Garth was quick to reassure her. "He's only here to try to identify you. Among other things, I don't want to be accused of kidnapping you."

Cara's face grew red and she closed her eyes in shame. She was going to be put on display like a horse at auction.

If he were in such a hurry to get rid of her, why did he not just take her to the public square for everyone to see?

Suddenly a new worry invaded her. It was highly unlikely, but what if somebody *should* identify her? Garth Stevens must not discover that she was Bart's sister. That would defeat her plan.

Once he had deposited her on the leather sofa, he walked into the hall, where the sheriff was waiting. "Come in, Mister Hicks. The young lady is in the library."

The short, middle-aged man stared at her while she assessed him, as well. His skin was a permanent brown, shriveled and leathery from too much sun. But his eyes missed nothing.

He turned to Garth and said, "Some men have all the luck...."

"Cara, this is Sheriff Hicks. He wants to ask you a few questions."

"Ma'am," the sheriff began, "I understand that you were knocked from your horse yesterday."

An instinctive respect for his ability warned her to be careful with her answers to him.

She kept her eyes lowered. "Mister Stevens said I did. But I...I don't remember."

"That's the big problem, is it not—remembering? Can you not recall who you are or where you were going?"

"No. I...I have such a headache, and the light..." Her voice dwindled to a whisper and she closed her eyes. She was afraid to look at him; for she was not a good liar. She felt the color spreading over her face.

Garth's voice engaged the man. "Has no one come to your office to report a missing girl?"

"No, and that's very strange. You would think the family would be tearing down the countryside, looking for her."

The voices grew fainter as the two men left the room. She was glad that she was not being asked any more questions, but she strained to hear the remainder of the conversation.

"What do you want me to do, Mister Stevens? I can send Jim Wilson for her and take her off your hands..."

"No, she's all right staying here," he quickly replied. "Dr. Coolidge said her memory will return once she gets over the initial shock."

"Well, I'll keep inquiring, Mister Stevens. There's a new group of refugees that came from Santo Domingo, but they're mainly French, and she doesn't speak like one of them."

"What about the horse? Has it been found?"

"No, but I really don't expect it to turn up. Too many people are eager to claim a stray horse."

At the news, Cara was relieved. Lady must have found her way back to the stables, where old Gregory would find her, remove her saddle, and put her out to pasture.

Chapter 5

*T*he sheriff had no sooner left when a carriage made its way into the yard. Garth, who had come back into the library, peered out the window.

"Brace yourself, Cara. Here comes a nosy neighbor of mine. I'm surprised that she let the sheriff get in ahead of her."

A few minutes later, a large, red-faced woman swooped into the library, followed by a shy young girl. The woman began speaking immediately.

"Garth, I heard what happened yesterday to this poor girl, with her clothes practically ripped off her. So this morning, I decided it was my Christian duty to bring some of Matilda's clothes for her to wear until her family comes for her."

Garth gritted his teeth but responded, "That's quite thoughtful of you, Mrs. Hinksley." He saw the woman's eyes darting to the sofa, as if she were waiting for an introduction.

"Mrs. Hinksley, this is the young lady. Cara, may I

present Mrs. Hinksley, my neighbor, and her daughter, Matilda."

The woman pounced on the name. "Cara? I was told that she didn't even remember her own name."

"She doesn't," he replied, "so I 've chosen to call her 'Cara' for now."

Cara's voice was soft as she spoke. "Thank you, Mrs. Hinksley, for the clothes. It's very gracious of you to lend them to me."

Settling herself in the nearest chair, Mrs. Hinksley said, "Oh, Matilda won't be wearing them again. In fact I was planning to put them in the missionary barrel—"

She suddenly stopped, realizing that she had said too much.

Quickly assessing the young woman as gently bred with probably a fine family, she said, "Garth, this girl's reputation is going to be ruined if she stays another minute unchaperoned in a bachelor's house. So I'll be happy to take her with me. She can share Matilda's rooms until her family comes to claim her."

"Madam," Garth's deep voice replied, "the girl is my responsibility and I will see to her care—no one else."

"Well, I must say, Garth, that you're taking a chance."

"How so?"

With a nervous laugh she continued, "Perhaps she hasn't lost her memory after all, but is out to snare a wealthy young man. Have you thought of that?"

Matilda blushed and looked at Cara in apology.

"You're mistaken, madam." Garth's voice had grown

cold and he was impatient at the exchange. "I doubt if any scheming female could will the limb off a tree to knock her unconscious at the feet of an eligible man. And now, I'm sure she's overtired…."

As Garth began walking to the door, Mrs. Hinksley took the hint. She departed promptly with her daughter following behind her.

When Cara looked up again, she saw Garth staring fiercely at her. Then suddenly he left the house, while calling to one of his grooms. "Henry, bring my horse around front immediately!"

Was he now regretting his decision? Did he believe Mrs. Hinksley — that she was a scheming female, setting a trap for him? His neighbor was right, of course. She *was* setting a trap, but not for the purpose the woman implied.

Cara closed her eyes. Eventually she drifted off to sleep.

A giggle coming from behind the sofa caused her to awaken. When she opened her eyes, two little heads disappeared.

"And who's hiding behind the sofa?" she asked.

Another giggle erupted and then a little dark face popped up. "Are you Miss Cara?"

"Yes, and who are you?"

"My name's Cookie," the little boy answered with a smile on his face. "And this is my sister, Tart."

When the second little face popped into view, Cara said, "My, my… Cookie and Tart. You both sound good enough to eat."

"My mama likes sweet things," Cookie explained. He turned to his little sister and said, "See, I told you it was like the sun and the moon streaked together."

"Are you talking about my hair, Cookie?"

"Yes'm. Tart wouldn't believe me when I told her what it looked like…"

Zellie's voice interrupted the conversation. "Cookie! Tart! You both got no business bein' in here, botherin' Miss Cara. Now, shoo! Out you go—back to your mama in the kitchen…"

"They're not bothering me, Zellie," Cara protested, but the giggling youngsters had vanished.

"Can I get you anything, ma'am?" Zellie asked.

"No, thank you," Cara replied, still smiling.

Left alone, Cara sat up, with her legs dangling while she waited for her head to assume its rightful equilibrium.

The room finally stopped spinning and she pushed herself to her feet. She surveyed the room, her eyes sweeping the empty space above the fireplace where a painting had once hung, judging by the slight discoloration of the wall. She noted the shelves of books, the massive dark mahogany desk standing at the far window next to the piazza.

Unlike the elegant drawing room, the library was a masculine room; one that a man would be comfortable in. But once again, her eyes returned to the puzzling empty space on the wall. What painting had hung there? And why was it now missing?

Her own godmother had been forced to sell many of her treasures. Was Garth Stevens also in need of cash? Perhaps he was not so rich as people believed.

But his fortune or lack of one was not the reason she had come. She was in his house to seek clues to the man's past. If she could get to the desk, could she possibly find some link to her brother's death?

All these questions were in her mind as she attempted the few steps to the desk. In her dizziness, she felt like an unsteady toddler learning to walk. Gratefully, she sat down in the desk chair. Opening the drawers silently, she found nothing of interest—but when she tried the last drawer, it was locked.

Only important papers were put under lock and key. And she needed to see what this last drawer contained. But where was the key?

Could it be upstairs in Garth's bedroom? That would be the logical place, would it not? But how was she to get upstairs and search, with so many servants in the house? She knew it was dangerous, but they all seemed to be busy elsewhere, and she had not heard anyone go upstairs for quite a while.

If Garth Stevens followed his usual schedule, he would not get back from the Exchange until late afternoon. So she could not allow this opportunity to pass.

Her bare feet made no noise across the polished floor, but it was taking her forever to get to the staircase. One step at a time... She was halfway up when once again dizziness assailed her.

"What are you doing, climbing the stairs by yourself?" Garth Stevens' furious voice sounded behind her.

She lost her balance and began to fall backwards, full force against the solid chest of the man who had shouted so angrily. They went down together and the breath was knocked from her, but he had broken her fall and taken the brunt of the hard steps himself.

"What's happenin'?" Zellie and James, the butler, came running toward them. "Lawd a-mercy. Are you both tryin' to kill yourselves?"

"No, Zellie. And we're all right," Garth assured her. "But we're going to have to watch this little wench more carefully in the future."

Chapter 6

Cara's efforts to search upstairs had been foiled. Instead, she was carried back into the library. While she was served a lunch tray in the library, Garth disappeared into the dining room to take his mid-day meal.

When he had finished, he returned to the library and settled himself at his desk. From time to time, he looked up from his writing to glance at Cara.

Properly subdued, Cara remained on the sofa and waited for Garth to leave. But he seemed to have no intention of doing so. If he remained at home for the rest of the day, then she would be unable to complete her search for the needed key.

"Mister Stevens," she began when he had put down his pen, "am I keeping you from something important? I know you have much to attend to, and I wouldn't wish to spoil your day."

"The men who work for me are well able to take care of things for one day. I have other chores that need my attention."

He rose and went to the window to gaze down the avenue of old oaks covered in Spanish moss. He seemed to be waiting for someone to appear.

Faint at first, the sound grew louder until the several carriages drew to a stop. Cookie ran into the library. "They's heah, Mister Garth. You told me to watch for them, and they's heah."

"Thank you, Cookie. Now run and help them to bring in the boxes."

A suspicious Cara asked, "Who has come, Mister Stevens?"

"Don't you think you can stop calling me 'Mister Stevens'?" he asked, frowning at her. "My name is Garth, and I would have you use it." But he did not answer her question immediately.

Only when some of the boxes appeared did Garth offer an explanation. "I should have been more aware of a young woman's needs, Cara, but it was only this morning when Mrs. Hinksley offered Matilda's castoff clothes.

"Belatedly, I realized that you could not remain forever in your riding habit. So I've engaged a dress shop to make a suitable wardrobe for you."

"But Mister Stev-" He glanced at her in a stern manner and she began again. "But Garth, I may not be here by tomorrow…"

He interrupted her. "On the contrary, I think you might be here for some time."

"No, I certainly won't. Besides, I can't accept a gift

from a man I don't know. It isn't…it isn't proper."

"Not even from your future husband?"

Cara laughed uneasily. "That's preposterous! You can't be serious. People don't marry strangers. And remember what Mrs. Hinksley said this morning."

The fiery flecks danced in her eyes in amusement. "I could be someone out to deceive you…someone who has gotten into your house under false pretenses."

She stopped smiling. "But let me assure you—I have no wish to marry you. I cannot accept these gifts."

A scowl crossed his brow. "You did not enter my house on your own. I was the one who brought you here. And while you are under my protection, you *will* be dressed properly, Cara. So we'll say no more about it."

On his way out of the room, he paused to speak quietly with Miss Barnes, the shop owner.

With the help of Cookie and James, the seamstresses went back and forth to the carriages, and when the room was littered with boxes and small trunks, Miss Barnes closed the door and gave her total attention to the embarrassed Cara.

She was measured up one side and then the other—arms, legs, shoulders—and then around every inch—waist, hips, breasts. There was no part of her body that had not been scrutinized and duly recorded in Miss Barnes' ledger hanging from her waist.

"Please…I need to sit down for a moment," Cara pleaded, after a length of time.

"Of course, my dear. I should have thought of that before." The woman's expression softened. "I understand that you had a bad fall yesterday."

"Yes."

While Cara leaned her head on the sofa, the two girls were busy opening several trunks, revealing gowns of pale, delicate materials—transparent Indian muslins and tulle—peasant hats trimmed with gauze, street hats, and various colored ribbons, flowers, and lace.

"Ordinarily, we would not have anything already made up," Miss Barnes confided, "but one of our best customers is as dainty as you are, and we had already started on some new spring and summer dresses.

"Although it's a little early to be wearing them, I think, with the heavier shawls, you'll be able to manage for the next few weeks. It will be scorching hot soon enough. Now, do you feel strong enough to try on several of the dresses, my dear?"

"Yes," Cara assented reluctantly, standing up slowly while holding on to the back of a chair.

"When is your wedding to take place?"

Cara started, then she understood. Evidently Garth Stevens was used to ordering lady's clothes. And the pretense of a betrothal merely saved the lady in question from undue embarrassment.

"I'm not... We— we have not yet set the date," she finished lamely, angry at herself for going along with the pretense.

"Well, evidently I expect it will be quite soon; for he

has given me the most beautiful fabric I've ever seen for your wedding dress, and wishes it to be made immediately. I understand he brought the material back from his last trip to Italy."

Cara remained silent.

The seamstress, Mariah, worked quickly, pinning the hem of one of the dresses to a proper length, while the other seamstress began sewing silk flowers to the short train of the pale yellow chemise dress.

"Well, at least we have a change of clothes for you until day after tomorrow," Miss Barnes said, "when we'll finish the others. But as for slippers, we brought only two pairs small enough to fit your feet. But that will have to do, until more are made for you."

Miss Barnes and her two seamstresses finally gathered up the remnants, the extra ribbons and hats, packed them in the trunks, and departed, while the finished dresses and accessories were carried upstairs to Cara's room.

Left by herself, Cara was still resentful of the way Garth had taken over her life, forcing her to endure the embarrassment and the pretense. Why, she had not even been consulted on any phase—not the colors, or choice of materials, or whether she had even wanted the dresses at all.

He had certainly wasted his money, since she planned to leave as soon as possible. Perhaps he could have the dresses altered for Maida. But then she gazed down at her own slender figure and realized that would be impossible.

In frustration, Cara picked up the ribbon left on the sofa and threw it to the floor. She wanted nothing from this man.

Chapter 7

Garth Stevens stood in the doorway of the library, with a strange expression on his face. "You've taken the afternoon well, Cara. Perhaps you'll feel strong enough to have dinner with me this evening. And I'd like for you to wear one of the new dresses."

He turned to leave, not waiting for an answer. It didn't seem to matter whether she wanted to do so or not. He had spoken and for him, that was enough. Oh, the insufferable arrogance of the man!

"Mister Garth," James said, coming in from the hallway, "there's a man out on the piazza says he wants to talk with you, sir."

The door to the house closed, and Cara finally relaxed. But then her uneasiness returned as she reflected on all of the activity of that day.

She had never been afraid of a man before. Many of Bart's friends had visited when she was at home from Miss Carey's School, and she had enjoyed their teasing—but Garth Stevens made her shake with fright. He was unlike the others, a much more formidable adversary, and she was anxious to finish her mission and escape as soon as possible. But for the moment, there was nothing to do but wait. And while she waited, drowsiness overtook her again....

"Cara, this gentleman says he knows you."

Her eyes flew open in alarm and she was aware that Garth was watching her closely.

Even though the man was dressed in fine clothes, he did not look like a gentleman. His eyes had a roving look that touched everything, and she instinctively reacted, sitting up in a rigid, frightened position.

"Ginny, sweet Ginny," the man began. He tried to take her hand but she recoiled from him.

"I've been so worried about you. When you didn't come back from your ride, I looked everywhere. It's a good thing that I heard you were here...."

How did he know her name, and why was he pretending to know her?

He turned to Garth and gave a twisted smile. "I'll take my fiancée with me now, Mister Stevens. And I'm much obliged to you for your trouble." He leaned over to help her from the sofa.

"No!" Cara cried.

With a scowl, Garth said, "Just a moment, sir! What did you say her name is?"

"Ginny...Ginny—Jones."

He knew her given name. Then he must know her surname, as well. So why did he not use it, instead of giving a false one?

"Do you recognize this man, Cara?"

"No."

"Well, it seems that's a problem, Mister Young. So do you have proof that her name is Ginny Jones—and that she is your fiancée?" Garth now positioned himself between Cara and the man.

"Mister Stevens, do you think I would come here to claim a stranger? My word as a gentleman should be sufficient..." He smiled the same twisted smile.

"I'm afraid it isn't, sir." Garth's voice was frigid. "I cannot allow you to take her."

The man's eyes glinted with malice. "I don't see how you can stop me. If you won't allow me to take her now, I'll be back to claim what's mine, rest assured." He turned and headed for the door.

"And rest assured, you will have to produce ample proof."

As if to protect her, Garth leaned over and took Cara in his arms. Headed for the stairs, he was holding her far too close, and her heart pounded against his broad chest.

Left in the bedroom, she was too troubled by the encounter to rest. Who was the man and what did he want with her? His appearance had been so puzzling. And she was unnerved at his threat. What could she do when he returned? Pretend that she had recovered her memory, and then challenge his story? Nothing was working out as she had planned.

A few minutes later, she heard the sound of water being poured into the brass tub in the alcove of the bedroom.

"Miss Cara?" A young, slender servant stood by her bed. "The master said I was to help you from now on. My name's Molly, and your bath is ready."

Basking in the warm water, Cara finally relaxed. The unpleasant experience downstairs was temporarily forgotten as the jasmine-scented soap and the water lapping gently against her body became a balm to her bruises. But too quickly the water became cool and she rose from the tub to be enveloped by the warmth of the linen Molly held out for her.

"Which dress will you wear tonight, Miss Cara?" Molly asked, opening the door to the large armoire.

"It really doesn't matter. Why don't you choose?"

Without hesitation, Molly selected the yellow chemise, embroidered with lilies- of- the-valley.

Once dressed, the stranger in the cheval mirror resembled Cara; yet she was different. The exquisite dress in the new Directoire fashion, with its high waist and deep decolleté revealed a figure that Cara had not known she possessed. Instead of a child, Cara saw a woman.

Molly, admiring her, said, "Now, Miss Cara, I'll tend to your hair. I'm good at that."

"Then, I'm glad. I've never been able to tame it, my-self."

Cara sat down at the dressing table, but when Molly began brushing the long strands, she winced.

"Am I hurting you?"

"You're very gentle, Molly. It's just that I have this bruise from my fall…"

Carefully Molly twisted the strands into a long coil on the top of Cara's head and fastened it with an ornament pin. Wisps of ringlets were allowed to spill over the tiny ears and caress the nape of her neck.

When she was finished, Molly stood back to admire her work. Her face broke into a grin while she commented, "After he sees you tonight, Mister Garth won't be lettin' *anybody* take you away from him."

She ignored Molly's comment and instead exclaimed, "Oh, Molly, I feel so much better. Will you walk with me down the stairs? I'd like to go out on the piazza for a while before dinner."

"I don't know. Mister Garth would really get mad if you fell again. The stairs are so steep. And then, in that dress, you might get chilled. It gets cold in a hurry once the sun goes down."

"I don't mind the cold, since I have the shawl. And as for the stairs, if you hold onto my arm and I'm quite careful, I should be able to get down safely."

Cara overrode Molly's reluctance, and she made it to the piazza without mishap. With nature's noise of the evening beginning on the banks of the river, she drank in the beauty of the gently rolling meadow and breathed the exotic perfume of the yellow jessamine that clung to the nearby trellis.

Nearer the piazza, clumps of azaleas, almost as tall as she, cast their budding glory into deep shadows, as the sun brushed its last brilliant strokes across the sky in shades of purple and gold. If only Bart were alive to enjoy such beauty! Things would be so different....

"Cara."

She turned to see Garth; satanically handsome — no longer dressed in the casual riding clothes of the day — but in a formal black waistcoat and breeches, and a frilled, snow-white shirt, studded with ivory.

At his frank appraisal of her, she lowered her eyes in embarrassment.

But he lifted her chin and forced her to look at him. Her eyes responded to his for one brief moment, and then the spell was broken.

"I see I haven't wasted my money." And with that, Cara once again remembered him as her enemy.

When dinner was announced, Garth said, "Can you walk the distance, or shall I carry you?"

"I can walk, thank you," she replied icily.

He held out his arm and they proceeded slowly across the piazza, but as soon as they reached the door of the house, Garth grew impatient.

"The food is getting cold," he said and, ignoring her protests, he swept her up in his arms, to carry her the rest of the way into the dining room.

Chapter 8

Struggling to regain some of her dignity, Cara sat in the dining chair he held for her. But she made no attempt at conversation. And having no appetite, she ate little of the food before her.

But aware of his dark scowl, she felt that she needed to defend herself. "Sir, I don't know what I've done to cause you to frown so at me. And I'm sorry that I've had to impose on you. But let me assure you that by tomorrow, I shall be gone."

"But you have nowhere else to go, Cara…except with your fiancé."

"Perhaps you would be so kind as to send word to Mrs. Hinksley that I will accept her hospitality…"

Garth threw down his napkin and stood up, muttering under his breath.

"What is this— a lover's quarrel so soon?" The young man, walking into the dining room, un-announced, was laughing.

"Calhoun, what are you doing here?"

"Why, Cousin, just coming to survey your latest acquisition. It's all over town that you're having young ladies drop at your feet these days."

Cara's cheeks burned at being spoken of in such a manner.

"Cara, may I present my cousin, Calhoun Wilkes. Cal, this is Cara."

An appreciative look lit up his face when he studied her. "Ma'am, if you're really considering changing abodes, may I offer you mine?

"It's a few miles downriver. The moss hangs lower; the wisteria blooms sweeter; the river's wider…and the welcome would be much nicer than my surly cousin seems to be capable of."

"Cal, I'm warning you…" Garth began angrily.

His cousin threw back his head and laughed again. "You'll find, young lady, that my cousin doesn't give up his possessions easily."

"Mister Wilkes," Cara replied, "I am no one's possession. I'm indeed unfortunate to be in such circumstances as to need a stranger's help for the present. However, I…" A tear slid down her cheek and fell onto the pale yellow dress. "If you will excuse me, I'm very tired."

Garth walked to Cara's side and offered her his arm. But she shook her head and said, "I can manage alone, thank you."

"No, cara mia. I think you require help for a short time longer." And with that she found herself once again in his arms. When he had reached the door, he turned around to speak to Cal, who had sat down to attack the piece of chicken James served him.

"Cal, are you planning to stay the night?"

"Why, thank you for the invitation, Garth."

"You're welcome to stay in the green bedroom."

"Not my usual one?" his cousin asked with a grin.

"Not this time. It's already occupied."

Later, in the upstairs bedroom, Molly came to help Cara undress. She slipped on one of the new nightgowns, but she could not enjoy the feel of the soft material against her body; for she could not forget the one who had purchased it.

I will not stay in this house another night, she vowed. But if it were to be the last one, she had only a short time to find what she was looking for.

With the sound of the men's voices downstairs, Cara decided Garth and his cousin would remain downstairs, leisurely talking over their peach brandy and in no hurry to get to bed.

So Cara slipped out of her own bed, took her candle, crossed the hall, and walked into Garth's bedroom.

The covers of the bed had been turned back and the doors to the portico were closed. The low embers of a fire still burned on the hearth.

In searching for the key, Cara ran her hand along the ledge of the mantel, then opened the doors to the two armoires, and finally moved on to the highboy.

There, in the last drawer, hidden under his shirts,

Cara found a small box. She felt two keys and was pleased. Perhaps one of the keys would fit the desk drawer downstairs. But just as she clutched the keys in her hand, she heard voices on the stairs. In sudden panic, Cara dropped one of the keys. It rolled out of sight under the highboy.

Put the other one back...Maybe he won't miss it, Cara told herself. But it was too late. Her escape was already cut off.

Quickly she dropped the other key, blew out her candle, and hopped into bed. The door opened a moment later, while the man with his own candle entered the room.

Cara kept her eyes closed but she could hear Garth moving about the room.

"Are you in such a hurry for me to bed you, my love?" He leaned over as if to kiss her.

Cara sat up with a cry. "Don't touch me! What are you doing in my room?"

"*Your* room? It can be yours if you wish it."

Cara pushed herself away from him and stumbled from the bed. She fled across the hall and once in her own bed, she put the pillow over her head to drown out his laughter.

Angry tears flowed down her cheeks. "Forgive me, Bart, for giving up so easily—but I can't bear to be in this man's house any longer. He suspects me now, so he'll watch and see to it that I find nothing to incriminate him."

Chapter 9

*T*he sun was coming up when Cara stirred. She climbed out of bed and pulled on her mended riding habit. Brushing her hair, she coiled it around her head and pinned it. Now for the boots... She frowned, thinking of the noise they might make on the stairs. It would be better to wait until she had reached the piazza before pulling them on. So she decided to carry them, instead.

That morning Cara felt much stronger and that was a good sign. Even the stairs were no longer a problem, especially with her carefully holding on to the railing. Since it would be much easier to slip out of the side door from the library rather than the massive front door, she entered the library.

Strange... The desk drawer that had been locked the day before now stood open. Did she dare look? Suddenly, she became afraid — not of getting caught, but in what she might find. Yet, wasn't this why she had come? She set her boots down and walked to the desk .

The only item in the drawer was a brown packet. tied with string. Opening it, Cara leafed through the papers until her brother's signature leaped out at her.

"Oh, Bart, did you gamble again, even after you promised?" His IOU for five thousand dollars stared at her.

She put the paper back into the packet, rewrapped the string around it, and pushed the drawer to its former position. Had five thousand dollars been worth a life to Garth Stevens? Sadly, she picked up her riding boots and walked toward the door.

"Did you find what you were looking for?"

Cara froze. "Garth?"

"I'm waiting for your answer, Cara. Or is it Ginny?" He reached out and grabbed her arm as she attempted to pass him.

"Let me go, you...you murderer!" Cara cried.

"So that's it, is it?" His grip tightened. "And whom am I supposed to have murdered?"

"Bartholomew Carter, my brother." She glared at him defiantly, despite his iron hard grip on her arm.

"And for what purpose, Cara?" He studied her face as if trying to fathom her reasoning.

"Perhaps for five thousand dollars?"

At that, he released her. "So you saw the IOU..."

"Yes."

"And you believed the worst — that I would kill for an unpaid gambling debt?"

"Yes," she repeated, but her voice had lowered.

"And is it your intention to get me hanged for

this so-called crime?"

Cara said nothing. Instead, she backed slowly toward the steps, while Garth advanced menacingly.

"You played your part well, cara mia. And I, taken in by your dramatics, believed you were really hurt." His countenance grew stern. "How could your parents allow you to come on such a fool-hardy venture?"

"My parents are dead," she said quietly. "And now, I wish to leave."

"I cannot allow you to leave, Cara." The voice was cold steel. "There is much you do not understand, but know this: I did not murder your brother."

His expression changed and his eyes narrowed. "Also understand that you are going to be taught a lesson you well deserve. No young woman enters a man's house alone, unless she is prepared to pay the consequences—whether as wife or mistress, I do not care. It's up to you."

"But surely, sir," Cara replied haughtily, "you would not wish to marry someone who hates you."

"Then, is it the other you wish?" he asked. "Perhaps I should have kept you in my bed last night." Once again, he gripped her arm.

Unsuccessful at freeing herself from his grasp, she she said, "Let me go."

"Never, my love. And if you attempt to do so, I shall call the sheriff and tell him that you are a thief who entered my home under false pretenses. Your fate would be a lot worse, I assure you."

"But I have taken nothing," she protested.

"Don't be so sure."

Preventing her from leaving, he swept her up into his arms and carried her upstairs to her bedroom.

"Your irrational behavior must be the result of your fall," he said sarcastically. "So for your own sake, I'll be forced to lock the door until I decide what to do with you. Molly will come and attend to you."

Cara heard the key turn in the lock as he left.

His words—"until I decide what to do with you—" were played over and over in her mind. He had given her two choices, each of which she found repugnant—wife or mistress. To her, one was little better than the other, except her humiliation would be complete if he chose the latter.

Downstairs, Garth paced back and forth.

He had deliberately frightened her. But he was aware that Cara was capable of stirring up a hornet's nest and had no idea what a vulnerable position she was in. The sudden appearance of the stranger and his threat to return could easily put her life at risk, and there was no one to protect her, except himself.

The day slowly drew out. Cara paced about the room in a daze, castigating herself for all the mistakes she had made and the repercussions to follow.

By mid-day, she went through the motion of eating, yet hardly knew what Molly had brought her. She ignored the servant's presence, preferring to remain silent, until finally, lethargy overtook her and she began to doze.

Both Garth and his cousin had been gone since morning, riding away together. But hearing the noise of their return, Cara awakened.

Riding boots sounded on the stairs. She heard the door unlock, and Garth, ignoring her, thrust a box into Molly's hands.

"Help Miss Cara put this on immediately," he ordered. Then he was gone.

Opening the box, Molly took out a shimmering white embroidered silk dress. "Oh, Miss Cara, I've never seen anything so beautiful…"

Cara stared at the dress. There was no mistake. It had to be a bridal gown. So Garth Stevens had made his decision. He intended to go through with his threat, but if she refused to wear it, would he actually send her to jail as a common thief? He was forcing her to marry him, and there was nothing she could do about it. She was trapped.

When she walked downstairs with Molly's help, Garth was waiting for her at the foot of the stairs. He watched while she descended to her fate. Her pale gold hair was entwined with orange blossoms, and the white silk of the dress moved in undulating rhythm, hugging her slim body with each step. Cara had the appearance of a sleepwalker, her amethyst eyes wide but unseeing.

To protect her from the cold, Garth draped a shawl about her shoulders and she took his proffered arm without emotion, to be helped into the waiting carriage.

Without conversation they rode, with only the

crunch of the carriage wheels on the sandy road to break the silence.

The avenue of moss-hung trees disappeared as they traveled toward a small white parish church with its spire pointing toward the sky. When it came into sight, the horses slowed and then stopped. Garth, turning to Cara, took his handkerchief and wiped a small smudge from her cheek, before lifting her from the carriage.

The parish priest greeted them and soon she was kneeling at the altar with Garth Stevens, the man she hated. As witnesses, Calhoun and another man she had never seen before attended them.

"Dearly beloved..." the priest began.

They were merely words, falling into the air. They had no meaning for her.

"...joined together in holy matrimony..."

Holy matrimony? How could it be holy? It was not a marriage, but madness—a holy madness...joined together in holy madness...

Then they were looking at her, waiting for a reply.

The sound that came from her throat was taken as a willingness to go through with this forced ceremony. The cup passed from her lips to his, and the sacrament was sealed. There was no turning back.

Unseeing and unfeeling, she was led back to the carriage, with the awful silence once more riding with them.

Garth watched Cara. He started to put his hand on her hand, but changed his mind and instead, laid his arm across the top of the seat.

Chapter 10

*U*pon their return to Mosshaven, visitors were waiting for them.

"Mister Garth," James said, opening the door, "that Mister Young and a sheriff's deputy are waiting for you in the library."

God! He had cut it close. He looked at Cara and seeing her face grow pale, said, "Cara, go into the drawing room and close the door. I won't be long."

Standing on the threshold of the library, Garth stared at the two men. "I understand that you wished to see me," Garth stated, eyeing the deputy with the assurance of a man accustomed to intimidate his adversaries.

They stood as Garth entered the room.

"Mister Stevens, b-beg your pardon, sir," the nervous deputy began. "This young man here— he…he came to Mister Hicks' office this afternoon, saying you refused to let him take his f-fiancée with him yesterday.

"Mister Hicks said you brought her here when she

was hurt in a fall from her h-horse... and that's what any good gentleman like you would do. I mean, to help a lady in distress.

"But since Mister Young is anxious to leave and the lady is better, I don't see any reason to k-keep her here. So will you please fetch his fiancée, so they can go on their way?"

"I'm afraid I can't do that."

"But Mister Stevens, if you don't g-give up the lady willingly..." He paused while he swallowed. "I'd hate to get a court order against you..."

"There is no law in the country," Garth replied in a deadly voice, "that would force a husband to hand over his wife to a stranger."

"What—what do mean?" Frank Young sputtered.

"Cara, or Ginny as you prefer to call her, is my wife."

At this information, the deputy seemed relieved. "You certainly w-wasted no time, Mister Stevens. She must be a b-beauty for you to act so fast." He inquired cautiously, "You have p-proof of the marriage?"

"Yes."

"Well, Mister Young, it looks as if your c-claim on the girl is no good. As Mister Stevens said—no law in the country will f-force a man to give up his w-wife...."

Cara sank into a chair, her knees no longer able to hold her up.

When the men had left, Garth found Cara shaking with fright and her face devoid of all color.

"Don't be afraid, Cara." He reached out to her, but

she brushed his hand away.

"Then, should I have allowed him to take you?"

"No. I don't even know who he is or what he wants."

"He wants someone named Ginny Carter." His voice grew stern. "If I am to protect you, even against your will, you must never mention your former name again — or that of your brother. To everyone you will be Cara Stevens, with no remembrance of the past."

Cara was confused. Was Garth frightening her into remaining silent about her brother?

One thing she did know for sure. If Garth ordered her to do something, she had little choice. She looked critically at her tall, handsome husband and saw a man who was used to being obeyed. His scowl alone was enough to send her into hiding.

"Come, Cara. We'll be dining upstairs tonight." He took her arm to guide her, and this time she did not protest. When they reached the master bedroom, he once again lifted her in his arms and this time, carried her over the threshold.

She warily looked around, seeing the four-poster bed that reached almost to the ceiling. The room and its furnishings seemed much more formidable in the twilight.

"This will be your bedroom from now on."

"But my clothes are in the one across the hall."

"No longer. I had Molly move them in here."

The little table near the upstairs portico had been set for supper, with a white linen cloth, fine Spode china, and heavy silver flatware.

Cara absentmindedly fingered one of the wine glasses before walking out onto the portico. She could almost touch the moss hanging from the tall tree that shaded the upstairs porch. The sun that had been so bright now sank from the sky, leaving the landscape bathed in shadows.

When she shivered, Garth wrapped his arms around her and said, "Are you cold, my sweet? I'll have James build a fire for you."

"No, there's no need." She would not let him know that she was cold with fright.

In a few short minutes, the mist from the river began to close in—a thick miasma, swallowing everything in its path. And the moss-hung oaks now assumed a more sinister shape, like grotesque giants swaying in the breeze, as if dancing a sarabande in a hypnotic rhythm. She felt surrounded by their presence.

It did not take long before the procession of food began—a wedding supper to be shared with her husband. James, Zellie, and Flora, another servant, carried in trays laden with delicacies. Silently, they placed the food on the table and then left.

Pouring the wine, Garth raised his glass to hers.

"To Cara, the cold sleeping beauty who holds a promise of fire..."

Cara lowered her eyes to avoid his insolent look, but she could still feel his eyes on her. Garth, seeming to enjoy himself, ate leisurely, while Cara toyed with her food. She drank little of the wine, but Garth had no such hesitation.

Finally he rose to pull the bell rope, and the servants were quick to clear the table and remove the trays to the kitchen.

When they had left, Garth said, "I'll send Molly to help you undress."

She blushed at his bluntness but gave no response.

"Take your time, Cara." He smiled at her and continued, "I have accounts to go over before coming to bed."

She glared at the back of his head as he left the room.

With deft fingers, Molly unfastened the wedding dress and helped her into the thin white gown that was designed to reveal the slender hips and legs, the soft curves of her breasts. Molly unwound her hair and brushed it into cascades of curls that reached almost to her waist. And when she had finished, Molly hung up the wedding dress and disappeared from the room.

Cara wiped the tears from her eyes. She was a wife—a married woman—and this was her wedding night. But the romantic ideals of the schoolgirl were now destroyed. Garth Stevens had married her casually as a punishment. And to show how little regard he had for her, he had gone downstairs to work on his books and ledgers.

Cara had always imagined a different wedding day, expecting to be married in the little white clapboard Presbyterian church in the Piedmont, where her late father had served as an elder. She had visualized being surrounded by family and friends, with a loving husband standing at the altar with her.

But that had not happened. The Low Country parish church had been empty, save for a priest she had never seen before, and two men who had served as witnesses—or guards. Both her mother and brother were dead, and she had kneeled beside a stranger—possibly a murderer—whom she had been forced to marry.

Suddenly Cara's heart beat faster. The giant of a man would come through the door at any minute, and she would be at his mercy. If she had loved him, or he had loved her, it would be a different matter. But Garth Stevens was her enemy, coming to do battle, and she was defenseless.

I will not submit! He had no right to force her. Anger swelled in her breast and she looked for an escape, but there was none.

Chapter 11

After an interminably long time, Cara finally heard his footsteps on the stairs. In desperation, she locked the heavy oak bedroom door and removed the key.

"Cara," the surprised voice called, "open the door!"

"No!"

"Cara, I will not have my own door locked against me. Open it, I say!"

She remained silent and still.

Garth gave forth with a terrible oath, and the door shuddered against his weight. Another shudder, and Cara could see part of the frame giving way. With a final, awful splintering of the wood, Garth was inside the room.

His face was dark with rage, but Cara stood her ground, glaring defiantly at him as he stormed toward her.

He stopped at the sight of the amethyst eyes blazing at him in anger. And then his rage gave way to an insolent arrogance.

In a mocking voice, he said, "And who is she that looketh forth as the morning, fair as the moon, bright as the sun, and terrible as an army with banners?"

He reached for her, but she stepped out of his way.

"Come now, do you think you're a worthy opponent for me? You should know that your battle is lost even now, before it begins."

"You have no right to—"

"I—no right?" His eyebrows lifted in surprise, and then amusement. "You don't seem to understand, Cara...You are my wife; you have no rights, except those I give you."

He was beginning to enjoy himself.

"If I should choose to beat you, no one would interfere." Barely able to keep the smile from his lips, he continued, "If I turned you out of my house, no one would plead your cause. "

The smile then gave way to a more serious look. "And when I say no door will ever be locked against me, you will do well to remember the consequences."

Cara gave a cry and put up her hand, but he crushed her in his arms until her soft breasts felt embedded in his chest. His mouth came down on hers with an insistence that alarmed her. And he carried her to bed.

"I had hoped to give you time, cara mia, to get used to me before...But I see that you would leave me if given half a chance. So the only way I can bind you to me is to make you truly my wife tonight...."

* * *

There was no fight left in her. She lay silently, crying, her cheeks wet with tears; not daring to move. Her mind and her body hated him for what he had done to her. He had taught her a bitter lesson, as he promised he would. Now, there was no doubt that he was the conqueror and she, for the moment, the conquered.

Garth tasted the salt on her cheeks and said in a gentle voice, "I did not intend hurting you, Cara, but your struggling against me only added to your discomfort. Don't be the wildcat, and it will be easier for you…"

He then drew the covers over them, and lay with his arms around her, his face buried in her hair.

But he had not finished with her. She was awakened in the middle of the night by her husband's lovemaking again.

When morning came, Cara awoke to find Garth watching her. "Well, my little passion flower, you're a handful; did you know that?"

Shocked at the desire in his eyes, she hopped out of bed. "Leave me alone, Garth."

He laughed and said, "It seems that you'll be getting a reprieve from my attention this morning. Although you're far more exciting than the rice fields, work has to be done today as usual."

Chapter 12

*T*he blinding headaches began that afternoon. Cara lay in the huge bed, moaning, as Molly and Zellie hovered over her, wringing cold cloths to place on her forehead in an attempt to ease the pain.

"James is gone for Mister Garth," Zellie assured her. "He'll know what to do...."

The boots bounded up the steps and Cara became aware of a man beside her, taking her limp hand in his.

"Oh, God! What have I done?" he cried out.

"Bart," she called in a weak voice.

"Cara mia, forgive me."

Garth remained by her side until the doctor appeared.

Conscious of voices talking in whispers, Cara could not decipher their meaning. The words were an untelligible jumble, sounding from a deep, dark tunnel, distorted and unfamiliar. She was once again entangled in her own special nightmare.

"Don't die, Bart! I'm trying to reach you... Mother,

do you think he'll come today? It's my birthday and he never forgets…"

She felt the coldness on her forehead and she shivered.

"I didn't want to leave—but the house was sold…I had nowhere else to go…."

She reached out. "You can't leave me, Brother…I'm all alone and so frightened…"

"I won't leave you," the voice beside her replied.

"No—I don't want to drink it," she protested.

The voice was persuasive. "Drink it for me."

She took a sip of the bitter drink and lapsed again into her own surreal world. "He frightens me, but I'll be brave. I'll see that he is punished for what he did to you…."

The man moved his hand, but Cara protested. "Don't take your hand away, Brother. I'm not afraid when I hold your hand."

For the next several days, Garth remained by Cara's side. She seemed so fragile, and he castigated himself for his earlier behavior toward her. But her hostility toward him had driven him to distraction. Now, she was the one paying for his own arrogance.

On the third day, Cara opened her eyes. Her headache was gone. She looked about the dark and silent room, seeing only a shadowed form in the chair beside her.

"I'm thirsty," she said in a weak voice.

Garth jumped up from the chair. "Cara! Thank God!"

"I'm thirsty," she repeated.

Garth lifted her gently to sip the cool water. And then he said, "Let me get Dr. Blondeau, my darling. He'll be relieved that you're awake."

He went out into the hallway and knocked on the bedroom door adjacent to the master bedroom. Soon, a tall, slender man was peering down at her.

"What...what happened?" Cara asked in a puzzled voice.

"You've been quite ill," Dr. Blondeau explained. "A delayed reaction from your fall. But now that you're awake, the danger seems to be over. In time, you'll be as good as new, but you must do nothing foolish to slow your recovery. A good long rest is in order for you."

He turned to Garth. "That goes for you, too, Garth. You must be exhausted from lack of sleep."

His attention was once more directed to Cara. She still had a puzzled expression on her face, and Dr. Blondeau attempted to explain.

"An injury to the head is a pesky business. No one knows whether, if you had remained in bed for a suitable time after the fall, you would have had this reaction or not. But I'm certain that your activity could not have helped, even though, in itself, it may not have hurt. But you're recovering, and that's the important thing."

Explaining further, he said, "It will be hard for you to remain inactive for the next few months, but that's the only way we can be assured of your complete recovery. Now, I'll leave instructions for your care, and will be back periodically to see you."

He glanced at Garth and then smiled at Cara. "You have a very persuasive husband, you know. I'm afraid my other patients have suffered from my neglect of them."

The days passed in pampered inactivity. Both Zellie and Molly attended to Cara through the remainder of February into March, past Lent and Easter.

Garth, who had reluctantly gone back to his work, seeing to the rice fields, the cotton, and the business of the Exchange, would sit with her in the late afternoons and evenings, reading aloud until she became tired and dropped off to sleep.

The nightmares had disappeared and Cara tried not to think of the role her husband might have played in the death of her brother.

The room overflowed with clothes—dresses that Miss Barnes had delivered while Cara was ill, but she wore only the gowns and peignoirs.

Dr. Blondeau came and went, and with each visit, he expressed pleasure at her recovery. But it was slow and tiresome for Cara, and she longed to leave the room that had been her prison for so long, and to sit on the piazza below.

Fanning herself with the fluted fan that Garth had brought her, she pushed her long hair away from her face. "I 'm so hot. I…I wish…"

Garth looked up with tenderness. "What is it you

wish, cara mia?"

"Could I...sit on the piazza—do you think—for just a little while?"

Garth closed the book he was reading. "Your world *has* been small," he admitted, looking about the room. "I should have been tired of one room long before now if I had been you."

"Then—you would let me?" She looked at him with pleading eyes.

He frowned. "Of course. You have only to ask, Cara. Do you wish to go now?"

"Yes." Her voice was subdued as she answered.

As he put his arms around her, he said, "You must eat more, Cara. You're far too thin."

He could feel her heart fluttering. Damn! Everything he said was too severe, too dictatorial. But he had to make sure that she recovered completely.

On the piazza, with the slight breeze surrounding Mosshaven, Cara began to enjoy the beautiful afternoon in the open, with the sounds and chirps of katydids and frogs around her. But much too soon, Garth said, "I think we should go back upstairs. You've been out long enough for the first time. I don't want you to get overtired."

She sighed, but did not protest.

Chapter 13

By April, the news of Mr. Jefferson's Louisiana Purchase had become the choice of conversation on every plantation; for with it, the dark clouds of war with France had been dispelled, and new avenues of commerce had opened up.

But that presented another problem. Pirates, not only on the seas but on the rivers, as well, were becoming more daring, and a worried Garth had lost several valuable shipments within the past few months.

But in the late afternoons, when he returned from town, Garth deliberately kept this problem to himself. Instead, he joined Cara on the piazza, to relax and enjoy a cool drink that James had ready for him, to rid the dust from his throat.

He continually brought Cara little presents— a music box, a set of watercolors—as if to make up for any pain he might have caused her earlier.

The strong, passionate man had now become gentle and tender in his effort to make amends for his earlier behavior. But what he had done when believing that she had tricked him and was not actually hurt was constantly between them—a fence as real as the one separating the rolling pasture from the house grounds. Still, Cara recognized that he had married her first, and for that, she supposed she should be grateful.

One afternoon, before Garth's usual arrival, a cloud of dust dispersed her thoughts as she enjoyed her time on the piazza. Cara watched as the fine phaeton pulled by two beautifully matched chestnut horses drew up and stopped in the circular drive.

She was delighted to see Calhoun Wilkes step out of the carriage and bound up the steps to her side.

Bowing low before her, he said, "I heard that you could have visitors, Cara, so I've come to see my lovely cousin."

She smiled at him. "Calhoun, I'm so glad to see you." Her eyes went back to the phaeton and the two matched horses. "What a beautiful carriage! Is it new?"

"Yes." He sounded pleased at her enthusiasm. "And when you're able to go for a ride, I'll come regularly...and if you're good, I'll even let you have a turn with the horses."

Excitement showed in her eyes as she stood near the railing to get a better look. "The horses are such beauties, and so well matched."

"Yes—I paid a pretty penny for them, I can assure you. Would you like to get a closer look at them?"

"Oh, yes, Calhoun."

He held out his arm. "At your service, ma'am," he

said, and together they walked down the steps.

The dust had hardly settled from Calhoun's arrival when Garth's appearance on horseback threw up another cloud.

Alighting from his horse, Garth immediately showed his anger at seeing Cara walking toward the carriage. "Cara, you're being foolish to be walking in the yard so soon."

Cara stepped back as if she had received a blow while Calhoun retorted, "You've guarded her far too long, Garth. Even Dr. Blondeau says she should become more active. Do you want to make an invalid of her? I've offered to take her for a drive as soon as—"

"She will go when I choose to take her and not before."

"Come now, Garth," Calhoun cajoled. "Do you always sound so angry at Cara? Have a care or your little linnet will fly from you when she gets her wings back."

Garth simply glared at his cousin.

With Calhoun's frequent visits, Cara began to display some of her earlier spirit that had seemed lost, and if Garth spoke to her a little too harshly, she responded with vigor instead of cringing as she had done in the past.

But she was still lonely and restless. So even Mrs. Hinksley and Matilda became welcome visitors.

"My dear, you'e looking much better than I expected," Mrs. Hinksley commented, greeting her one afternoon. "But still too thin…Matilda, take these benne cookies to Zellie and tell her that I made them for Miss Cara—to help fatten her up."

"How kind of you, Mrs. Hinksley."

In her usual brusque manner, the older woman leaned toward Cara and asked, "Have you ever gotten your memory back?"

Before Cara had time to answer, Mrs. Hinksley answered her own question. "But of course not, since your husband still calls you 'Cara'...yet, I think it quite strange that no one ever came forward to claim you, except that awful Mister Young.

"Let me tell you, he left town in a hurry, or so I heard. The sheriff couldn't prove it, but he decided you had been kidnapped by that man, and somehow you had escaped him. Lucky that Garth found you when he did."

Her eyes widened at the confidence she was waiting to share. "People in town say you had such a terrible experience that it would be better if you never recalled what actually happened to you...

"But still, there are some mamas who would have given their eye teeth for their daughters to have been in your place. So romantic for Garth to have married you—and surprising, too.

"I thought surely the young Widow McAlistair would get him to the altar first. She has that fine plantation next to his, you know...."

When Matilda returned to sit with them, Mrs. Hinksley became silent on the subject.

"Will you have some lemonade, Mrs. Hinksley? And

perhaps we might enjoy some of your delicious cookies," Cara suggested.

"Well, now, it *is* awfully hot."

Cara rang the bell and when Zellie came onto the piazza, she said, "Will you please bring a pitcher of lemonade for us and some of the cookies that Mrs. Hinksley made?"

They had almost finished the tall, cool drinks when Garth rode up on horseback. Although dusty from the ride, he remained outside with them for a few minutes. At that time of day, he would have liked something stronger, as James well knew, but with Mrs. Hinksley present, he accepted the glass of lemonade that Cara poured for him.

It was not long before Mrs. Hinksley stood up. "Matilda and I really must be going. It's getting late and Mister Hinksley will be looking for us."

"I'll walk you to your carriage," Garth offered.

"Good-bye, Mrs. Hinksley—and do come again. Good-bye, Matilda," Cara called.

After helping mother and daughter into their carriage, Garth came back to Cara with an amused look on his face.

He leaned over and gave her a light kiss. "You have made another conquest, my sweet. Mrs. Hinksley approves of you."

Cara giggled, the dimple showing in her right cheek. "It's because I approved of her benne cookies. What else could she do?"

* * *

With Cara's continued improvement, Garth was now away even more of the time, using his tremendous energy to build up his holdings, and to supervise every phase of his plantation and his business in town.

"I'm not like the absentee landlords, Cara—spending my time in gambling and other idle pursuits, and leaving everything to the care of the overseer. My family lost much during the War, and it has taken years to rebuild. The rice fields were unattended and our indigo crops destroyed." He paused for a moment and then continued.

"It was just as well—about the indigo—for there's no market for it now. But this new black seed cotton..." His eyes lit up. "It promises to make a fortune. That is..."

"Does the...the Widow McAlistair grow black seed cotton, too?"

"Where did you hear that name?"

"Oh, Mrs. Hinksley just happened to mention..." Cara let the rest of the sentence hang in the air.

"I suppose she told you that I 've been looking after Margaret McAlistair's plantation while she's away?"

"No."

"Well, it's true that I've been going over to check on the overseer. But he's a man who knows what he's doing. Still, Margaret feels relieved, knowing that I'm watching."

"How old is she?" Cara asked.

"Margaret? She's two years younger than I am—twenty-six."

"And does she have children?"

"No—none." Garth looked at her, frowning. "Why all this sudden interest in Margaret McAlistair?"

"I…I was just curious about my neighbors."

"Curiosity seems to be a habit with you." His voice took on a teasing manner. "It's gotten you into trouble more than once, has it not?"

Cara bristled, but didn't answer.

"Curiosity is not always bad," he acknowledged. "In fact, I'm curious as to when I'll ever see my final shipment from Italy. It 's been some months now…."

Chapter 14

Garth did not have long to wait for the treasures he had purchased from abroad. The day the wooden crates arrived, he was in a festive mood.

"Cara, there's a very special painting I saw when I was in Italy. Although the price was dear, I had to own it. If you feel up to having guests, I 'd like to invite friends here for the unveiling.

"Zellie and the other servants can see to the refreshments. All you'll have to do is to look like a very beautiful wife, as you do now…"

"I'll be happy to help with the invitations, Garth. At least, I can do that."

So she was to be acknowledged after all, before his friends. And he evidently expected her, as a true wife would, to act as hostess.

As they walked upstairs, Garth had his arm around her. He lingered at the door of the master bedroom, but then quickly leaned over to kiss her on the cheek before he went into the opposite bedroom.

Molly was waiting to help Cara with her dress. On the bed, she had laid out a long blue gown with matching peignoir. While Cara stood, waiting to slip the gown over her head, she remarked, "Molly, I think I need more exercise. Or perhaps I'm eating too much. My stomach seems to be getting a little bulge."

Molly smiled and said, "Well, babies has a way of doin' that to you, Miss Cara...."

Cara's flushed face emerged from the folds of the gown, and she stared at Molly in surprise.

"But I didn't tell you I was expecting..."

"You didn't have to, ma'am. I could read the signs. Especially in the mornin's."

A stunned Cara lay in the darkness. It had not occurred to her that she might be with child so soon. But then, remembering the wedding night, she realized that it was possible.

Keeping the secret to herself, with only Molly as her confidante, Cara continued her routine as before, resting and being cared for, until the evening arrived for the unveiling of the painting.

A knock sounded at the door just as Cara stepped from the tub. She quickly threw on her peignoir as Molly opened the door. Garth, her husband, with a special evening gown over his arm, entered the room.

"I would have you wear this tonight, Cara...and I've given Molly instructions as to how to style your hair."

Surprised at his request, Cara examined the dress, which was hauntingly beautiful. The material, of finest silk, was a deep pink with flecks of gold. Transparent sleeves fit the upper part of her arms and from her elbows, the material cascaded down like fluttering doves. Gold plaited trim crossed her breasts, and the same trim became the rope about her waist.

Her white shoulders, against the color of the material, took on a porcelain glow of rose petals, and the skirt, falling in flowing lines, embraced her shapely legs. It was an ethereal dress, almost too beautiful to be real. It seemed made of the fragility of flower petals, with golden streaks of stardust.

Once dressed, she sat at the small mirrored table, where Molly took the rope of tiny seed pearls and pale pink silk flowers and wove it into her hair. And when she was finished, Molly left the room, to be replaced by Garth, with his look enveloping Cara.

His eyes spoke of passion and latent memory burning deep within him. He came to her quickly and, searching the deep, amethyst eyes, he smiled and held out his arm for her. "Come, Cara. Our guests will be arriving soon."

The first to appear was Calhoun Wilkes. He bowed low before Cara, taking in her appearance as if overwhelmed. "Madam, if you are in the room when Garth's masterpiece is unveiled, the poor painting will be completely ignored."

"Mister Wilkes," Cara responded, smiling at him, "you always did have a flatterer's tongue, but everyone has come to see this painting that Garth has raved about for so long. And I, for one, can hardly wait."

Soon other people began to arrive. The Reverend

Pinckston, with his wife and three daughters, was followed by Matilda and her mother and father. And then Garth moved from Cara's side to greet a tall, slender woman who had just stepped from her carriage.

Garth had seldom showed such courtesy as he offered his arm to help her up the steps. "If I had known that you were in the marrying mood, Garth, I would not have stayed away so long," she said, looking at him with her soft, brown eyes.

Overhearing the exchange, Cara felt as if she were suddenly an outsider.

"Cara, may I present Margaret McAlistair, our neighbor — My wife, Cara."

"How young you look," the woman said. "In fact, much too young to take on the responsibility as mistress of Mosshaven."

Cara, outwardly ignoring the sugar-coated barb, smiled sweetly at the widow. "I'll learn eventually, Mrs. McAlistair, with Mister Stevens to help me...and I hope, perhaps, that I might call on you for advice."

Garth stood back, his eyes twinkling. Cara knew that the interplay was not lost on him.

Then she became busy, greeting other guests who had come from up and down the river and from town, making them welcome. Through it all, she felt as if she were merely a participant in a drama. So that night, Cara thought only of playing the part well that Garth had assigned her — as mistress of Mosshaven.

Tables had been set up on the piazza, and all the

house servants were busy, carrying dishes, trays and bottles of Madeira and peach brandy. Once when Cara glanced toward the tall azaleas at one side of the house, she thought she saw Maida, but then the figure disappeared.

Poor Maida, thought Cara, not to be included in the festivities. But with a question directed at her, she thought no more of the overseer's daughter.

"Will you be going into town for the social season, Miss Cara?" one of the young gentlemen asked.

Not knowing what to say, she glanced at Garth, who answered for her. "I don't think so, Huguely. We will more than likely remain here at Mosshaven during the summer."

"A pity," the young man replied. "You're already a legend in Charleston—the beautiful, mysterious Venus that the gods dropped from the sky to grace our midst." He sighed and went on to flirt with the unattached females who were sitting at the far end of the piazza and giggling behind their fans.

"But aren't you afraid of Cara's catching malaria, especially in her weakened condition?" a solicitous Mrs. Pinkston asked.

"She'll soon be as strong as ever," Garth replied, "and besides, I'll give her some of the bark to stave off any chills."

"Cara will have to learn, Mrs. Pinkston," the Widow McAlistair added, "that she can not run off at every opportunity to engage in light amusements when so much needs to be attended to. I'm also planning to stay this summer at my plantation—Sussex Hall."

She looked at Garth, waiting for his reaction, but he was watching Cara daintily consuming the barbequed chicken, rice, pickled peaches, little snow peas, and Flora's famous spoon bread.

Cara looked up to meet his questioning glance, smiled at him and continued to eat, finishing off the vanilla cake that Zellie and Flora had whipped up that afternoon.

With her appetite, Cara knew that she would not be able to keep her secret much longer.

Later, when the guests had finished eating, Garth finally stood and invited the group inside to the library. The room became crowded, with a few standing together at the double doors leading into the room.

With his hand resting on Cara's back, Garth began speaking.

Chapter 15

"When I was in Florence, Italy, I saw a beautiful, intriguing painting in one of the old palazzos," Garth informed his guests. "I went back time and again to gaze at it—so often that it became an obsession. I wanted it, no matter the price. But the owner refused to sell, since it had been in his family for more than a hundred years.

"Disappointed, I traveled on to Venice, to Rome...to all the places where tourists usually visit. But I could not get the painting out of my mind. So I traveled back to Florence. I found the owner, who was quite old, in poor health, but he welcomed me again. And convinced that I would always honor the painting, not just for its value but for its beauty, he allowed me to purchase it. But it was not to be shipped to me until after his death.

"A few weeks ago, I received word that the painting was on its way. So, ladies and gentlemen, may I present *The Cara Mia* by Bellicini...."

Garth removed the linen drapery. The impact of the

painting was immediate. The guests gasped and then began applauding.

From where Cara was standing, she could not see the painting because so many people had crowded around it for a better look. But all at once, the room became silent as the guests' attention turned from the painting to Cara.

Seeing the painting for the first time, Cara also gasped as she looked at her own image. Dressed in the same pink silk with pearls and flowers in her hair, Cara mirrored the fragile, faraway look of the girl on the canvas.

Calhoun's voice broke the silence. "It would be mighty cold to bed a painting, Garth." He laughed. "Lucky for you that you found someone who resembles your dream."

The full impact of his comment hit Cara and, with a little cry, she rushed from the room. Up the stairs she ran, not stopping until she reached the master bedroom. How could Garth do this to her in front of so many people? She tore the pearls and flowers from her hair and pulled the smothering dress from her body and threw it on the bed.

She was nothing but a fantasy for him. He had even called her by that name the moment he had seen her. All this time he had desired, not her, but the ageless beauty captured on the canvas.

It was obvious too, to all his friends, and she felt her humiliation complete.

Cara opened the armoire to find another dress — the

lavender tulle that she had planned to wear in the first place. But when she opened the door, something alive slithered out to coil at her feet. In horror, she stared down at the diamond-backed snake, and a scream escaped her throat.

Not knowing that Garth had followed her, she heard his warning voice as he shouted, "Don't move, Cara!"

She willed her body to remain still as Garth moved toward her. In a rapid maneuver he struck the rattler with his coat and then crushed the head of the snake with the heel of his boot.

The sound evidently penetrated the house because a short time later, Calhoun was at the door. "What is it, Garth? What's wrong? I thought I heard Cara scream."

"It's all right, Cal," Garth assured him. "There was a lizard in the room, and you know how squeamish women can be at the sight of a harmless creature."

"Well, if that's all…"

"It is, Cal. Will you please go back and assure the guests that all is well. We'll be down shortly."

Cara remained in Garth's arms while he comforted her.

"Is it…dead?" she asked.

"Yes. But it certainly ruined one of my best coats," he replied, deliberately making light of a near tragic situation. "I'll have James remove the snake immediately."

Remaining in the bedroom, he did not mention the pink dress on the bed. Instead, he helped Cara redress in the lavender tulle and waited for her to repair her hair. Then the two went across the hall for Garth to select another coat to wear.

When they returned downstairs, the group, seeing Cara in another dress, decided that the original dress had been part of the couple's plan in highlighting her similarity with the painting.

For the rest of the evening, Garth did not let Cara out of his sight. Although she remained pale, she smiled and continued to play her part as hostess. And when the guests were taking their leave, she stood beside Garth to bid them good-bye.

"It was a lovely evening." the minister's wife said to Garth. Leaning over to Cara, she whispered, "You have him bound twice to you, my dear. It's not often that a wife can control her husband's dreams, too."

After the last guests disappeared, Cara and Garth walked upstairs. But Cara hesitated at the door of the master bedroom. "Do you think it's…?"

Garth nodded. "James promised to see to it. But if it makes you feel safer, I'll doublecheck."

She sighed in relief and stepped into the bedroom with Garth at her side. The serpent was gone, with only a small telltale sign on the floor.

Molly, who came into the room to help Cara, said, "Here, Miss Cara, let me unbutton your dress for you."

"Thank you, Molly. I think I could go to sleep standing up," she said, stifling a yawn.

Garth sat languidly in the easy chair, watching as

Molly helped her mistress get ready for bed. He made no effort to leave and Cara, disconcerted that she had no privacy, turned her back to slip on the gown.

When she moved to the dressing table for Molly to unpin her hair and brush the strands falling loosely down her back, Garth said, "Molly, you may go." He took the brush from Molly's hands and the maid disappeared.

Cara's scalp tingled, not from the sure, quick strokes of the brush, but from Garth's presence beside her. He had the power to stir her and it made her uncomfortable as he put down the brush and caressed one curl in his hand.

"I was proud of you tonight, Cara. You made all our guests feel welcome. I hope we will have many nights such as this…"

She looked at his reflection in the mirror and then lowered her eyes. She felt ashamed at her angry display of temper at being dressed like the girl in the painting.

"Everything went well," Garth continued, "except for one small unpleasantness…." His voice had become deep and husky. "And because of that incident, I think I should stay with you tonight."

Cara did not protest.

The covers had been turned back and the thin mosquito netting unhooked from the sides. Garth helped her into the tall bed, closed the netting and then left for the other bedroom to undress.

While she was alone, Cara pondered the strange, frightening event of the evening. She knew that the snake had not crawled into the armoire on its own. And she distinctly remembered closing the door to the armoire before going downstairs. So it must have been placed by someone who wished to harm her after she had gone downstairs.

Garth returned from the other bedroom, blew out the light, and lay down beside Cara, who warily moved to the edge of the bed. But Garth made no attempt to touch her. Instead, he went to sleep with his face toward the door.

Chapter 16

When Cara awoke the next morning, she found her arm lying across Garth's bare chest.

"Good morning, Mrs. Stevens," Garth said. "And how does the lady of the house feel this morning?" He leaned over, touching his lips to her hair.

Cara stretched lazily and retorted with a smile, "I had such a pleasant dream. There was a most handsome man, with dark hair and a broad chest..."

Garth scowled.

"...He stepped from his portrait with an awful scowl and slipped into my bed during the night."

Garth chuckled and playfully slapped her leg. "You little hussy..." His hand remained, then moved slowly to caress her thigh, and came to rest over her stomach. There was a flutter and he gazed at her in surprise.

"Are you already hungry after eating so much last night?"

"No. I'm afraid the baby is protesting his father's hands," she responded softly.

"Oh, my God!" He jerked his hand away as if he had been burned. "There's no mistake?" he asked.

She shook her head. "No…none."

He sat up on the side of the bed. "I had not wished for a child so soon…."

She was hurt at his reaction to the news of the baby, and because of it, she lashed out at him, "I'm not exactly thrilled either, to be bearing your child."

He turned to her and his face was so dark that she thought he might strike her. Instead, he stood up, wrapping the sheet around him, and left the room.

The anger that Garth showed wounded Cara. Most men would be pleased. Well, sir, she said to herself, you should have thought of that possibility on our wedding night.

Poor, unwanted baby. Despite what she had said to Garth, she was glad to be with child; for she had lost everyone else that she truly loved, except for Sonia, her godmother. Yet, she was faced with the unhappy thought that her baby would be born with only one parent's love.

But if that were so, then she would have to accept the responsibility. She must forget Garth's admission, however hard, and now that it was no longer a secret, she needed to begin making plans for the baby's arrival, which she had put off.

A layette, a cradle, a furnished nursery — these were the needs of all babies. Although she was passable in sewing the simpler things, she hoped that Garth would not object to her hiring Miss Barnes, to help make a few of the more complicated baby clothes. And then the baby would need a cradle and a suitable nursery. In such a large house, there must have been a room set aside for a nursery. But where? She would ask Zellie later; for she certainly would not bother to ask Garth.

That afternoon, when she had the opportunity, she questioned Zellie first about a cradle.

"Yes'm, there's a family cradle—sturdy and strong. It's stored in the attic, jes' waitin' for another generation. I rocked Mister Garth in it myself, when he was a baby, and Mister Evers, too."

"Evers? Who is that?"

"Why that's Mister Garth's baby brother."

"But why has he never spoken of him? Is he still living?"

"Yes'm, Mister Evers is...but he and Mister Garth had a fallin' out after their mama died, and Mister Evers say he never comin' back so long as Mister Garth's alive."

"How awful! What did they fight about?"

"Well, you know what a terrible temper Mister Garth has—although he's been mighty nice while you been here. But you ain't seen nothin' 'til Mister Garth gets riled up.

"He spent all summer a-workin' and a- worryin' about his cotton. First, the weather was too dry...Then, it was too wet. But finally the cotton was ready to pick—a nice big crop.

"Anyway, Mister Evers was supposed to see to it that the fine sea-island cotton was put in the warehouse, when Mister Garth was away. But instead, Mister Evers went to play cards. The cotton was delivered, but had to be left outside, 'cause Mister Evers, he had the key to the warehouse and the men couldn't get in.

"A powerful storm came up and all that fine cotton, a whole season's worth, was ruined. When Mister Garth returned and found out what had happened, he horsewhipped Mister Evers in front of everybody on the wharf."

"And Mister Evers left home because of it?"

Zellie nodded her head. "That he did—lock, stock, and barrel."

"How long ago was that, Zellie?"

"Almost three years ago. Let's see…Mister Evers is about twenty-two by now."

"Why, he was just a boy, then."

"Yes'm. That's what I tried to tell Mister Garth…that he was mighty hard on 'im, so young—but he wouldn't listen. It caused a lot of hard feelin's in the family. Miss Lutie, the aunt who lives in town, sided with Mister Evers. He went to live with her and he don't have nothin' to do with Mister Garth now."

"And in these three years, did they never see each other?"

"Only once, that I know of, and even then, it almost turned into a fight."

Throughout lunch, Cara kept thinking of this

young brother-in-law and felt a kinship with him; for they had both experienced Garth's wrath.

To alleviate her distress, Cara tried to keep busy. She went to the attic with Zellie to view the baby furniture and, with Molly's help, they decided on the pieces to be brought down and refurbished for the nursery.

Cara had so many things to think about. She really needed to write each item down so she could remember them. But she had no pen or paper.

Would Garth be angry if she used some of his from his desk in the library? She decided to risk it.

She had avoided the library ever since the unveiling of the painting. There was something eerie about seeing her own face from another time. She did not like to be reminded that she was a substitute. If it had not been for her resemblance to the painting, she would be safely away from Mosshaven. Instead, she was being taught a lesson that Garth Stevens could have anything he desired, and that she was powerless to stop him.

When she walked into the library, despite her dislike of the painting, her eyes were drawn to the mantelpiece and the painting. But something was wrong.

Shocked, she saw that Garth's painting had been slashed. What a travesty! Who could have done such a thing to a priceless work of art?

She walked closer to view the damage. On the hearth beneath the painting lay a knife. It looked familiar, and so she picked it up and turned it over to examine it more closely, trying to recall where she had seen it before.

"Madam, if you value your life, you will put the knife down before you do further damage."

She whirled to face her husband standing in the doorway.

"But I—"

"Will you please leave this room?"

"Garth," she protested. "Let me explain…"

"Madam, the evidence speaks for itself. You have chosen well in your effort to punish me."

He would not listen and, in despair at the animosity in his eyes, she dropped the knife and ran crying from the room.

Chapter 17

Cara remained in the bedroom and did not go down to supper. She was too upset to eat. How could Garth have thought her capable of such an action— damaging a valuable painting, even if she disliked being reminded of the reason he had married her?

The supper tray that Zellie sent to her was returned to the kitchen, uneaten. By the next morning however; she was ravenously hungry, and she quickly devoured the food on her breakfast tray. During the day, she walked in the gardens and cut some of the flowers to take back to her room.

She did not see Garth and he made no effort to seek her out. And the second night ended much like the first.

Later, on the next day, to pass the time, she took out the watercolors that Garth had given her earlier and, as she began painting, she longingly recalled her happy days spent at Miss Carey's School with her best friend, Elsine.

What a pair they had made! Cara smiled as she recalled the subterfuge the two had perpetrated while students.

"Oh, Ginny, if I could only do watercolors like you! But mine run together and come out so muddy. I wish you could show me how you get such beautiful, transparent colors. I have no talent at all...."

"Elsine, stop berating yourself. Why I've never seen anyone sew a finer sampler, or do a neater stitch than you. I envy you your sewing. Mine's so terrible that I spend more time removing stitches than putting them in. But wouldn't it be lovely if I could paint watercolors all the time and you could do the samplers?"

Elsine's eyes began to sparkle. "Ginny, are you thinking the same thing I am?"

"You mean—I finish your paintings for you and you finish my samplers?"

"Would that be so frightfully wicked?" Elsine asked, giggling.

"It would be just what old Pruneface deserved."

How they got away with it, Cara would never know. Yet, she and Elsine had received prizes at the end of that year. Of course, Elsine had received the top prize for the best sampler, but Cara had gotten an award for the most improvement. And as expected, Cara received the award in watercolors, with Elsine taking a minor prize.

Cara, remembering those days, looked down at the picture she was painting, and her only regret was that

Elsine would not be beside her, helping her with her sewing of baby clothes.

It had been three days since the episode in the library. During all that time, Garth had not sought her out. Boredom finally set in, as she grew tired of painting. And since there was no pianoforte in the house, there was little left to amuse her.

Feeling restless, she longed for— not a simple stroll in the gardens—but a fast gallop on a horse...to feel the wind against her face and the wild freedom of going wherever she wanted to go.

In all the clothes that Garth had ordered for her, Cara did not have a replacement for her riding habit. If the mended one she had worn on that fateful ride were still in the armoire, then she would need to wear it again.

Pulling out clothes and accessories, she finally found it in the bottom drawer. It still fit her except for a tightness at her waist. But most important, it was still wearable.

Cautiously descending the staircase, Cara slipped out of the house and headed for the stables. Once there, she began to look for a sidesaddle that she could use, as well as a horse that would not be too difficult to handle.

Luckily, she had not come across any of the grooms; for Garth might even have left instructions to them not to let her mount. As Cara wandered down an aisle of stalls, one of the horses whinnied as she walked by. She stared up at the beautiful black horse with a white patch on his nose.

"Oh, you beauty," she cried, and the horse came to nuzzle her cheek.

Everything she needed was hanging beside the stall—everything except a saddle. But surely Garth's mother had ridden, so there must be a sidesaddle somewhere. She finally found one in the tack room and carried it back to the stall.

As she led the horse to the mounting block, she said, "You look as if you need a gallop, too."

He was spirited and a little frisky, perhaps for not having been ridden in several days. But she calmed him with her slow, sure movements.

It felt good to hold reins in her hands again. She trotted around the riding ring, getting used to the horse and soothing him with her sweet voice.

"Miss Cara! Mister Garth don't want you ridin'…"

Cara ignored the voice and galloped away.

Oh, how good it felt to be riding! The beautiful black horse, given his head, flew down the road. The pins fell out of her hair, and she could feel the long strands playing in the breeze—almost as if she, too, had come alive with newly found freedom.

She forgot her cares, her unhappiness, and Garth's harsh words. She became one with the horse. But then the breeze died and the air became stifling, so she slowed to a trot. It was then that she became aware that she was thirsty and she knew that the horse was probably thirsty, too.

Cara turned into the wooded glade along the creek

bank and jumped from the saddle. The horse drank from the cool, spring-fed stream, and then Cara tied his reins to a sapling in the shade. Following the stream, she found the spring and dipped her cupped hands into the cool water again and again, until she could drink no more.

It was so cool and peaceful by the creek. But it was getting late, and Cara knew she needed to make her way home. If Garth found out about her ride — and he probably would — he would be quite angry. Since he was already angry with her, however; she decided it would not make much difference.

Using an old log to step on, she mounted and turned the horse out of the glade. The sand on the road was deep, and little swirls of dust drifted up, making her cough.

Soon, the summer rain would begin, and although it would cool the landscape and help the cotton growing in the fields, the rain would also fill the stagnant pools in the swamps, with the accompanying danger of malaria.

Cara had not gotten far on the sandy road when she saw another horseman kicking up a larger swirl of dust in the distance.

Chapter 18

$\mathcal{A}$s the horseman approached, Cara recognized Garth. Coming immediately behind him was a landau, driven by Henry. And when Garth saw her, he appeared relieved, but his words were severe.

"I should have thought that you knew better than to be riding in your condition, Cara. I shall have to see to you more closely until the child is born. It seems you don't give a care to the danger to either you or the child."

Cara said nothing.

"Come, you've been on horseback for too long. You're to ride the rest of the way home in the landau."

He jumped from the bay he was riding and taking the reins of both horses, he led them to the back of the carriage to tie them there.

He lifted Cara from the saddle, holding her close to him for a moment before helping her into the carriage.

As Henry guided the landau home, Cara, sitting beside her husband, said nothing. She was not going to apologize. She was glad she had gone riding since she felt a lot better by doing so.

The silence was finally broken as they rode along the avenue of old oaks approaching Mosshaven.

"Cara, your things are being packed. After we have dinner, I 'll be taking you into town."

She remembered his words earlier: "If I should choose to turn you out of my house, no one would plead your cause..."

Cara gave a little cry. "Do you hate me so, that you would make me leave, even when I'm carrying your child? What am I to do? Where am I to go?" Tears filled her eyes at his cruelty.

"Cara, you do me an injustice. I'm merely taking you to my house in town so that you can be better cared for. You'll be closer to Dr. Blondeau. Also, I don't want you at Mosshaven during the malaria season. Because of the child, you cannot take the bark."

"I...I did not know that you had a house in town." She brushed away an errant tear.

"There are many things that you don't know about me." He continued, "Molly will be with you, as well as Henry and Flora. And Flora will be taking Cookie and Tart with her. Zennia and Russell, who usually take care of the town house, will attend to you, too, of course. James and Zellie will remain at Mosshaven."

Still thinking of the cool glade, Cara said, "Won't it be unbearably hot in town?"

"I think you'll find it comfortable. My house is built of wood, not brick. And although it increases the danger of fire, at least wood does not absorb the afternoon heat like brick. It helps that the kitchen is separate from the main house and that a cool evening breeze blows in from the Atlantic."

"Where…where will you be?" asked Cara.

"I have business to attend to and will be leaving for London soon. When I return, I'll divide my time between Mosshaven and the town house."

"Will the baby be born in town?"

"Yes." He did not comment further and Cara was hesitant to ask him any more questions.

When the landau arrived and came to a stop near the steps, Garth climbed out of the carriage to help her into the house. Noting the mended riding habit, he said, "After the baby comes, I see that you'll need a decent riding habit to wear."

With no further conversation, Cara walked upstairs to take a bath and change clothes. She found Molly busy packing for her removal into town.

"I left the blue muslin dress out for you to wear tonight, Miss Cara, if that's all right."

"Thank you, Molly."

When Cara had dressed, she found Garth waiting for her in the hallway. And for the first time in three days, they walked down the stairs together and entered the dining room.

"The riding seems to have agreed with you," Garth admitted.

"It was wonderful to be back on a horse again. Why, that big black beauty of a horse seemed to have wings. With the wind in my face, it seems that I could have flown to the ends of the earth!"

Garth laughed at her exuberance, but then sobered. "But poor Henry got quite a tongue-lashing when I found out you had ridden that one. He's such a spirited horse that I was afraid you wouldn't be able to handle him.

"But Cara," he said, his eyes imploring her, "promise me that you won't do such a foolish thing again—for your sake as well as the child's. After the baby comes, I'll buy you a gentler horse more suited to you."

Surprised that he seemed to be concerned for their child, she replied, "I promise."

During the course of the meal, Garth asked, "How soon can you be ready to leave?"

"I have only a few things to get together, but Garth…" She hesitated.

"Yes, Cara?"

"If I'm not allowed to ride, are there any books to read at the house in town?"

"Some," he replied, "although not as many as we have here. Do you have any particular ones in mind?"

"I've always enjoyed Shakespeare—especially *The Taming of the Shrew*."

He laughed out loud. "Select any you want to take with you, Cara."

"Thank you, Garth."

Later, when she walked into the library, her eyes were drawn to the mantel over the fireplace. She saw that the painting had been removed.

Her attention returned to the books, but she could

not read the titles above the first shelf. So she climbed the library ladder to get a better look when Garth walked into the room.

"Cara, do I have to watch you all the time? It's dangerous for you to be on the ladder."

"Then, how do you expect me to get the books? I can't reach them without the ladder."

A strange expression came over Garth's face as he looked first at her and then to the mantel over the fireplace. Standing on the ladder, Cara was only as tall as the mantelpiece, itself. His eyes betrayed his relief at that sudden realization.

His voice became tender. "Come, cara mia—I 'll get them for you." And he held out his arms to help her down from the ladder.

Chapter 19

*T*he carriage laden with trunks had gone on ahead with the servants' carriage. Garth took the books and other small personal items to put in the landau and, with one last glance, Cara left Mosshaven behind.

Although there was a slight breeze, the air in the landau was warm. They had not gone far before Cara, tired from her afternoon excursion, was lulled to sleep by the steady sway of the carriage. In a protective gesture, Garth put his arm around her, with her head resting against his chest. Her jasmine-scented hair loosened and blew in tantalizing strands across his cheek, undermining his determined restraint.

Finally, the carriage finished its silent journey.

"Cara." Garth's voice spoke softly in her ear. "Cara, we're here...."

Her eyes flew open and she gave a little start. Not cognisant of where she was at the moment, she pushed away from him.

He caught her arm as she became off-balanced.

"I 'm not an ogre, ready to eat you," he said gruffly.

"Since you seem to have a habit of falling, I suggest that you not be so quick to shun assistance."

He stepped from the landau and, shame-facedly, Cara fell into his outstretched arms.

Russell, the houseman, waited with a light at the door.

Cara managed a drowsy "Good evening, Russell," and continued to be guided by Garth. Her dark, amethyst eyes, wide but unseeing, blinked at the light as Russell led the way into the town house.

"I told the other servants to go on to bed and not wait up for us. So do you think you can manage without Molly for tonight?"

"Yes," a still sleepy Cara answered.

The lamp in the bedroom was lit and Garth went out with Russell. Later, when he returned, Cara, fully dressed, was curled up on the daybed, asleep.

"Oh, my little sleepyhead, what am I going to do with you?"

By morning, when the sun shone through the window, Cara awoke. Looking around the strange bedroom, she remembered almost nothing of the previous evening, except for a vague feeling of being helped out of her clothes. But it was Garth's hands she remembered, and not Molly's.

As she gazed about her, her mood lightened. There was a difference, not only in the ambiance of the room, but a decided change in atmosphere. The oppres-- siveness of Mosshaven had disappeared and she actually felt happy for the first time in months.

She had not realized how unsure of herself she had been at Mosshaven, always wondering what new hurt was in store for her. She had been apprehensive ever since the day Garth had threatened her, ever since he had promised her no mercy. Though he treated her kindly at times, she always remembered the threat.

First, her illness had provided a temporary lull in his paying her back for her deception. And now, since she was carrying his child, she had somehow won a second reprieve. If he were incapable of loving the baby, at least his male vanity would insure his wish to sire a strong and healthy child.

As Cara looked down at her rounding stomach, a tremulous flutter began. An over-whelming love swept over her and she put her hands upon her stomach, to feel through her fingertips the new life within her.

But after the reprieve, what would be the future of this child? Would Garth give the baby its rightful place as heir to the Stevens name and wealth? Oh, he would provide the necessities, but a child could not flourish in an atmosphere of indifference. It would be up to her to change his indifference to love. But how? What could she do?

With sudden insight, she realized the terrible task ahead of her. Only by becoming the loved and adored wife of Garth Stevens could she hope to sway him. She must put away her anger, her hate, to persuade him to love her, and later, their child.

But how could she accomplish this if he would not even share the same room with her? She certainly could not announce to him, "Garth, I 've decided to become your loving wife so you will love our baby."

Instead, she would have to show him in small ways, at first. And that meant swallowing her pride and starting anew in this new house. She consoled herself that it would not have to last long, since he was leaving soon for London.

A sudden longing for a papaya interrupted her thoughts. She had become increasingly a slave to her appetite, and it didn't matter the time of day or night.

Putting on a dressing gown and, with only a few strokes of the brush on her long, tangled hair, she walked toward the dining room. Garth, sitting alone at the table, rose to greet her. "I'm surprised to see you up so early this morning, Cara. I know that yesterday was quite tiring for you."

She gave him a dazzling smile. "I must have gotten a good night's sleep, sir; but I woke with a terrible yen for a papaya. Do you think there might be one in the house?"

"I'm afraid not." He smiled at her indulgently. "Would an orange do for now?"

At her nod, he selected an orange from the fruit bowl and sliced it with his knife. Watching him, Cara frowned. The knife with the strange handle was a replica of the one she had found near the damaged painting. But how was that possible?

As he handed her the plate of sliced fruit, Zennia came into the dining room. "Would you like your cup of tea now, Miss Cara?"

"Yes, thank you, Zennia."

Garth, who had finished his breakfast rose reluctantly from the table. "Do you think you'll be all right alone, Cara? I have much to take care of today."

"Of course, Garth."

At her second smile of the morning, she could see the startled look on Garth's face. Finally, he left the dining room as if he did not want to go, yet not daring to stay.

Cara was delighted with the house. She went over it from top to bottom, admiring the fine, polished pieces of furniture, the silver and crystal chandelier that hung in the upstairs drawing room. She was fascinated to see that the chandelier lowered from the ceiling for the candles to be replaced, and then could be drawn up again.

The Aubusson rugs on the floor were magnificent and Cara, unused to such luxury in recent years, marveled at the expense of furnishing the town house in such a grand manner. Although Mosshaven was well furnished and comfortable, it could not compare with this jewel of a town house.

The day passed quickly, and by late afternoon, when Garth returned home, he found Cara sitting by the enclosed courtyard pool.

She was not aware that he was observing her as she lazily swished her hand in the water and watched the little fish swimming back and forth between the lily pads.

"You're quite lovely in the afternoon sunlight," he

said, coming to kneel beside her and taking her hand in his.

She looked into his searching eyes. "Thank you," she replied and then asked, "Did you finish all of your business today?"

As she waited for his answer, she tried to ignore the pulsating feeling that traveled up her arm from his touch. But she did not withdraw her hand to break the spell.

"Almost everything. I've made amends with Aunt Lutie Cowper and we're on speaking terms again. I had not told you that my aunt and I had some differences several years ago…"

"Zellie told me," Cara interjected.

"Well, since I'm to be away for several months—"

"That long?" Cara asked, her voice quivering.

"Yes. The ship sails in three days." His lips brushed her hair. "If you were not with child, I would take you with me. But since that's not possible, I did not wish you to be here alone, without a female relative. So I've made arrangements for Aunt Lutie to look in on you from time to time."

Cara stood up, breaking the intimacy and shaking the water from her other hand.

"I've also made arrangements in the shops," Garth continued, taking his handkerchief from his pocket to dry her hand, "for you to purchase anything you might wish while I'm away. My solicitor will provide funds for you while I'm away, and Calhoun will help you if you need him."

"Thank you, Garth." Cara knew she should be grateful that he had evidently provided well for her in his absence. "I...I shall miss you," she said in a small, shy voice.

"If that were only so, cara mia," he murmured.

The magic of the garden took over and Cara pushed aside the moments of hate to indulge in the sunlit dream. Acting as if she were a real wife, loved by an adoring husband, she lifted her lips to his and he, incredulous at her action, drank from them as a thirsty man from a cool spring in the desert.

"If you're not careful, I might miss the ship to Liverpool," he said.

They walked back inside. But anyone who had observed the two in the garden would have assumed that they were very much in love.

On the next day, Garth announced, "I've accepted an invitation to a supper party tonight on Legare Street. I don't care much for the dancing, but it's time that you had some fun."

"But Garth, what will people say...My condition..."

"It's not that obvious yet, especially if you wear one of the high-waisted dresses." He caressed her shoulder and stared at the rising, full breasts. "No one's eyes will get as far as your stomach...."

Cara's face turned pink and Garth was amused.

So they were to take part in the summer social season—at least until Garth left for London. And in her excitement, Cara could not make up her mind as to which dress to wear. Finally, Molly settled it for her.

"You can never go wrong with this one, Miss Cara. It makes your skin look like milk and honey."

And so she wore the white gown that bared her shoulders, with her only ornament the circlet of flowers surrounding the coil of golden hair.

"You're very wise, my dear, not to burden yourself with fancy jewelry," her hostess greeted her, indicating with a sweep of the hand all the older women laden with their diamonds, emeralds, and pearls. "Nothing should take away from perfection, itself."

Then the woman turned to Garth. "You're to be congratulated, Garth. Where did you find her? On your doorstep, was it not?"

"No, Miss Julia. It was in an enchanted glade among the wood creatures, who're still crying for their lost Titania," he exaggerated.

Miss Julia laughed in appreciation. "Ah, and I see that she has woven a spell over you, too. Take care that you don't wake up to find her stolen by some renegade Puck. I've heard that more than one has thought of it."

Garth registered a flicker of annoyance at her remark, but then he smiled at his hostess and escorted Cara into the ballroom.

The two joined in a cotillion for the first time that Cara had ever danced with her husband. She was aware of the attention they were getting, but Garth gave no indication that anything unusual was happening. Perhaps he was used to being the center of attention, but for Cara, so recently a schoolgirl, it was an unsettling but exhilarating experience.

During the evening, they moved easily from the supper table to the small groups of people clustered around the room.

Garth knew everyone, and surely it was out of politeness that so many of his friends asked her to partner with them in the dance. But he did not seem pleased when she was singled out for a waltz. When the evening was only half over, he strode up to claim her. "I think we should leave, Cara. You're beginning to look a little feverish."

Puzzled and hurt, Cara said nothing, but allowed herself to be guided by Garth to Miss Julia to bid her good night.

On the way back to East Bay Street, they sat silently in the landau. *It will be hard to get him to love me,* thought Cara. But she must keep trying.

Chapter 20

*T*hat evening, when Garth and Cara reached the town house from Miss Julia's party, Garth hurriedly said good night, leaving Cara to Molly's care, while he remained in the library before finally retiring to his own bedroom.

By the next morning, when Cara awoke, Garth had gone, and she spent a lonely day, except for a time in the garden with Cookie and Tart. The only activity occurred in the late afternoon when a delivery cart arrived.

"A man just brought a basket of papayas, Miss Cara," Russell informed her. "Said Mr. Garth ordered them for you. Do you want me to take them to the kitchen?"

"Oh, yes, Russell. And will you please tell Flora that I would like one with my breakfast tomorrow?"

Cara smiled to herself at Garth's thoughtfulness,and she renewed her determination to get him to share her bed before he left for London.

That night she dressed carefully for dinner, in the pale yellow chemise dress that she had worn the first evening she had dined with Garth at Mosshaven. And although it had been a lovely little dress before, her fuller figure gave it a sensuality that it had not possessed at the first wearing.

All through dinner, Garth did not take his eyes from her—from the moment she had first thanked him for the papayas to the final bite of chocolate mousse. She was the coquette, looking up at him in what she hoped was an alluring manner.

"Russell," Garth said, getting up from the table, "I'll have my brandy in the library."

"Yes sir, Mr. Garth. And Miss Cara, will you have anything else, ma'am?"

"No, thank you, Russell. But do tell Flora and Zinnia that the dinner was delicious."

"I'll do that, ma'am."

Garth laid his hand on Cara's forehead. "You still look a little feverish, Cara, as you did last night." His eyes showed concern for her.

She blushed; for she knew the real reason for her hot brow. What could one expect, she thought to herself, when a woman was trying to seduce her husband to sleep in the same bed with her?

"I...I feel fine, Garth."

"Your face is flushed, cara mia. I don't like the signs. I think I should have Dr. Blondeau come around tomorrow. And I don't think you should be up any longer. Come, I'll help you to your room."

"But your brandy…"

"It can wait."

He went as far as the door with her, then leaned down to kiss her on the cheek. "Good night, Cara." Without looking back, he descended the stairs to the brandy waiting for him in the library.

Cara stamped her foot in anger. She could not even seduce her own husband. Walking to the highboy, she snatched up the first gown she touched. It didn't matter that it had no real substance to it. Molly would be the only one likely to see her in it.

Cara had already unhooked her dress and put on the gown when Molly entered.

"You shoulda called me, Miss Cara. I didn't know you were getting ready for bed so soon…"

"It doesn't matter, Molly. The dress was easy to slip out of…" She sighed as Molly took up the brush and began the evening ritual of brushing the long strands of golden hair.

When she had finished, Molly said, "Do you want the light on for a while?"

"No. Please blow it out."

Cara lay in the darkness, the breeze coming in from the French doors to the balcony. Wide awake, she watched the patterns on the ceiling, changing from the light from the carriage house to the moon glow silhouetting the tree leaves.

Suddenly, she heard a noise from the balcony and a large moving shadow crossed the ceiling. With a cry, Cara leaped from the bed and ran down the stairs.

Garth rushed out of the library. "What is it, Cara? What has happened?"

"Someone...someone was trying..." She gulped. "Someone tried to get into my room."

"But no one has gone up the stairs. The door has been open...I would have seen..."

"From the balcony...I saw him on the balcony."

"Who, Cara? Whom did you see?"

"I...I don't know."

Russell appeared then. "Mister Garth, is there somethin' the matter?"

"My wife thought she saw someone on the balcony. Get Henry and search the grounds."

"Yes, sir!" He immediately ran out the door.

Garth took the stairs two at a time. But a short time later, he returned, having found no one in the bedroom. He started toward the front door, but Cara clung to him.

"Don't leave me, Garth. Please don't leave me..."

He looked at the small, frightened figure beside him and, for the first time, he noticed the thin, flimsy nightgown and bare feet.

"Well, I can't very well take you outside like that. I guess we'll just have to stay here and let Russell and Henry take care of any intruder." He smiled as if he did not really believe that she had seen someone.

Garth took his coat to put around her, and when Russell returned, he was still holding her in a protective manner.

"We didn't see anybody, Mister Garth. Me and Henry searched good, but there's not a trace…."

Garth nodded. "Miss Cara was a bit feverish tonight, and I expect she just had a bad dream. It was probably no more than a shadow from the trees."

"Yes, sir. I hope that's all it was."

"You may go on to bed, Russell. I won't need anything else tonight."

"There *was* someone," Cara said softly to no one in particular. "I saw him, even if no one believes me."

"Do you think you can go back to sleep, Cara? I'll be across the hall if you need me."

"Don't make me stay alone tonight, Garth. I'm too frightened."

He hesitated and his eyes grew hard. "I thought you didn't like sharing your bed with anyone."

"Just for tonight. I won't ever ask again."

He entered the room with her and went to the balcony to look out.

"Please lock the doors," she begged.

"It's too hot with the doors closed, Cara. I'm sure that no one will try to come in, but if you're that frightened…"

He did not finish his sentence, but let her know by his manner that it was a great concession for him to close the doors on a cool sea breeze and to share the same room with her.

Cara, already in bed behind the mosquito netting, could hear Garth in the dark as he stripped off his clothes and climbed into bed beside her. He lay close to her, breathing heavily.

Finally, he turned to her in frustration. "You are asking too much of me, Cara — to be beside you and feel your warm, velvet flesh... without...without doing anything about it."

He moved and she could feel his strong, naked body against hers. She put her trembling hand upon his chest. "I...I would not deny you...your husbandly rights, Garth, if...if you do not hurt me."

"Oh, my sweet..." His lips found hers and he was gentle in his caresses, while Cara responded....

When she awoke, she was still in his arms. Immediately, she moved away from him. But as he got out of bed, his manner was arrogant and amused.

"So my little ball of fire has cooled this morning..."

She groaned in dismay and pulled the sheet over her head.

"Don't be embarrassed, my love. I'm pleased not to have a cold hag for a wife."

He left the room and she could hear him across the hall. Pulling the bell rope for Molly, she said, "I'll have breakfast downstairs this morning. But first, I need a bath."

By the time she walked into the dining room, Garth had finished his breakfast.

"Good morning, Wife. You had a comfortable night, I trust?"

Blushing, she replied, "No, it was not particularly comfortable at all. There was a lump in the mattress and I fear I'll be black and blue for some time from it."

He laughed aloud.

Russell brought Cara's papaya to the table, just as Dr. Blondeau announced his arrival.

Garth got up to greet him and bring him into the dining room. "My wife felt feverish last night," Garth explained, "and I thought you should have a look at—"

He got no further. Flora came running into the dining room, crying. "Oh, Mister Garth, somethin' terrible has happened to Cookie! I think he's dyin'!"

Dr. Blondeau and Garth followed Flora to the kitchen. Cara rose, too, then sat down again. She knew she would only be in the way.

With her thoughts on the sick little boy, she absentmindedly picked up the knife and sliced the papaya into sections, removing the black seeds. Just as she raised a slice to her mouth, Garth rushed into the dining room and knocked the papaya from her hands.

Seeing the look on his face, she asked, "Garth, what is it?"

"You didn't eat any of it, did you?"

"How could I, when it fell on the floor?"

"Thank God! I think the papayas are poisoned, Cara. That's what's wrong with Cookie. He ate one this morning."

She gasped. "Will he be all right?"

"Dr. Blondeau is working with him now to get out the poison."

"But how? How could they have been poisoned?"

"It's easily done," Garth replied. "In a number of ways."

"But why? Why...?"

"I have no way of knowing. More than likely, it was an accident and perhaps just one was poisoned. But to make sure, the others will be destroyed."

He stooped to pick up the piece of fruit from the floor and then he took the plate with the remainder from the table.

Still shaken from the episode, Cara went into the library where Russell came in with her fresh cup of tea.

"Cookie's goin' to be all right, says the doctor, but he's still a mighty sick little boy." Russell was shaking his head. "And that Mister Garth was so beside hisself when he found out it was the papaya that done it, knowin' you were eatin' one, too. If anything had happened, I'da never forgiven myself."

"You had no way of knowing, Russell," Cara replied. "Besides, I never tasted it, because—" She was suddenly interrupted from a voice in the hallway.

"I knocked on the door, but no one ever came. Is it always this disorganized? I thought Garth would manage better than this."

Cara, seeing the plump, middle-aged woman walking toward her, said, "Aunt Lutie?"

"Yes, my dear. And you must be Garth's wife, Cara."

"Do come in, Aunt Lutie." Cara stood up. "I'm sorry, but we've had a frightful scare this morning. Cookie, the cook's little boy, was accidentally poisoned, but he's going to be all right. Luckily, Dr. Blondeau was in the house."

"If there's a doctor in the house, he should be look-

ing after you. You don't look at all well…far too pale."
Aunt Lutie clucked her tongue.

"I'm fine. Will you have a cup of tea, Aunt Lutie?"

"No, thank you, child… spoil my lunch." She waved
Russell away. "I see why Garth came to visit me.
Menfolks don't know a thing about caring for a
woman who's expecting. He should have sent for me
long ago. Oh, there you are, Garth," she said, seeing
him standing in the doorway. "Why haven't you taken
better care of your wife? I declare she looks like she's
going to pass out at any minute."

"Cara has been ill, Aunt Lutie. I told you about the
fall. And we've had some excitement this morning."

"That's just what an expectant mother doesn't need,"
the woman snapped.

"Yes, Aunt Lutie."

Cara was amused. Garth seemed just as subdued
under his aunt's admonishment as he was by Zellie.

Although she protested, Cara was put to bed for the
rest of the day by Dr. Blondeau. So her shopping trip
had to be postponed. And Aunt Lutie, satisfied that
Cara was being taken care of, went back to her own
house, with a promise to return the next day.

But by late afternoon, Cara was determined to get
out of bed. "Molly, please come help me," she
requested. "It's so hot that I'd like another bath."

When she was dressed, she started to the library to
replace the book she had finished reading. Voices in the
drawing room alerted her that Garth had returned
home.

"Tilt it a little to the right, Russell. Yes, that's much better. Thank you, Russell."

She smiled as she passed the servant in the hallway. But before she reached the library, she saw Garth standing at the entrance to the drawing room and surveying the space above the mantel. She, too, glanced toward the mantel, but her eyes narrowed as she recognized the restored painting, the *Cara Mia*.

"How can you allow your precious painting to remain in the same house with me? Are you not afraid that I'll slash it again?" a sarcastic Cara asked.

"I think it appropriate for my two treasures to be together in the same house. Besides, I was hasty in accusing you. You might have had the intent, but you were too small to accomplish the task."

"And when did you decide that?"

"It doesn't really matter," he replied, dismissing her question.

"You know I hate it. Why do you torture me by hanging it here in this house?"

He towered over her. "However you feel about the painting, I expect you to take care of all my possessions while I'm away—my painting, my child—and everything else that is mine."

"Oh, you are insufferable!" Her eyes blazed as she turned to leave.

He caught her arm. "You didn't think so last night," he murmured, his voice hoarse.

"That will be the last invitation to my bed, I assure you."

"I do not need an invitation," he replied. "As you so clearly stated last night, I have a husband's right."

He released her and she fled from the room.

Cara decided that it had been a mistake to act the loving wife. Why degrade herself by trying when she had no hope of getting Garth to love her? But at least, if the ship sailed on schedule, she would be free of his overbearing manner for the next few months.

Suddenly, Cara thought of Cookie. What would make him feel better? He had been slow to recover from the poisoning, and she knew he was missing all the activities at Mosshaven for the summer.

She remembered how much he had enjoyed watching the frisky little brown colt running about the pasture, and his interest when she had done the watercolor sketch of the colt.

So Cara located the sketch to give to him and started across the courtyard. She looked around, but saw no one. Yet, she had this strange feeling that she was being watched. That had happened often since her fall. Now, she was beginning to wonder if the falling limb had addled her brain more than she realized, making her imagine things.

"Flora, I've brought Cookie a little present. I hope he's feeling better."

"He's better than he was this mornin', Miss Cara, but he's just lyin' there, still as can be. Not like my Cookie at all. He'll be pleased you come to see 'im, I know."

"Cookie," Cara called softly. "I've brought something for you."

A slight, pathetic little smile greeted her.

"It's a picture of the little brown colt at Mosshaven. Do you remember that day that I sketched him? And see, that's you — sitting on the fence."

She held up the picture and his smile grew wider, while his little hand reached out.

"I never had a picture like this before. That sure is good of Frisky."

"Is that what you call him?" asked Cara.

Someone else entered the room. When Cara looked around, she saw Garth.

"Mister Garth! Mister Garth! Look at my picture Miss Cara drew for me."

Garth came closer and peered down at the watercolor. "That's a fine picture, Cookie."

"Yes, sir. It looks just like Frisky — and see, that's me sittin' on the fence. I never had anything this fine before. Don't you think Miss Cara's the best picture drawer you ever did see?"

Garth smiled. "Yes, Cookie, she's a fine picture drawer. And you're a very lucky fellow to have a picture drawn for you. Perhaps she'll draw one for me some day."

He turned to look at Cara and she hurriedly said, "I must go, Cookie. I hope you'll feel better soon."

"I'll walk with you," Garth commented.

As they crossed the courtyard together, Garth remarked, "It seems that you have many talents that I'm not aware of. If I had known you were that good, I would have gotten a larger set of watercolors. But that can be remedied."

"It was merely something to pass the time when I was ill," Cara said with a shrug.

When they entered the house, Garth turned to her. "I almost forgot why I was looking for you. Do you feel well enough to dine with Aunt Lutie tonight? I had hoped on this last night to dine at home. But I dare not refuse her invitation. She's determined to make it a total family reconciliation," he added in a dry voice.

"Is your brother—?"

"Yes. He's back from his last sea voyage. I can't say that I'm looking forward to the evening. I would much rather…" He stopped, seeing the relieved look on her face.

She knew that there was bound to be a certain amount of tension at Aunt Lutie's, but at least she would not have to face Garth alone at the table. Besides, she was curious to meet her brother-in-law.

"Henry will be in front with the landau in one hour," he remarked, a coldness coming into his voice. "I don't like to keep the horses waiting in the street, so do try to be on time."

Chagrinned that he seemed to be able to read her thoughts at times, Cara was determined not to be upset by his sudden animosity. But her face had been too revealing. As she climbed the stairs, she realized she must learn to hide her feelings if she were to survive.

Chapter 21

*O*ne hour later, Cara descended the stairs, the aqua gauze dress floating about her and concealing her rounded stomach in its folds. Again her only ornamentation was the rope of silk flowers binding her pale gold hair.

Garth, waiting at the foot of the stairs, caught his breath. When she reached the last step, Cara hesitated; for there was something arresting about her husband's careful scrutiny.

"Come with me into the library, Cara. I see that your dress leaves something to be desired."

Cara bristled. She had spent only as much time as he had allowed her in getting ready.

"I'm sorry that you're not pleased with my appearance, but I thought it more important to be on time, since you made it clear..."

He saw the hurt in her eyes. "I didn't mean to give the impression that I'm not pleased."

He led her to the safe in the library and pulled out a small chest. He opened the lid. "Here is what you need to complete your wardrobe." And with that remark, he pulled out a strand of the most exquisite pearls that Cara had ever seen.

"Turn around," he ordered, and she quickly obeyed.

She felt his hands fastening the pearls at the back of her neck and, against her will, a shiver pervaded her body. She turned quickly and her cheek brushed his face, still bent low over her.

"Thank you, Garth, for allowing me to wear these tonight," she whispered.

His arms enclosed her and he gazed deeply into her eyes. "I am not *allowing* you to wear them, Cara. They are yours to do with as you wish."

His mouth came down suddenly on hers and she could not breathe for her own emotion.

"Please," she gasped, "Molly will have to start all over if—"

He released her and once again became the distant husband. "Of course, and it's time to leave."

Garth helped her into the waiting landau, and a short time later, they arrived at Aunt Lutie's tabby brick mansion.

"Good evening, Jasper," Garth said to the butler at the door. "My aunt is expecting us."

"It's good to see you again, Mister Garth. Miss Lutie's waitin' for you in the drawin' room."

Aunt Lutie's greeting was cordial. "I'm so glad that you both could come tonight." She took Cara by the hand and guided her to the other man in the room.

"Cara, this is your brother-in-law, Evers Stevens.

He's just arrived home from a voyage around the world. Evers, meet your new sister-in-law, Cara."

The young man had stood when Cara entered the room, and she could see that he was almost as tall as Garth, though not quite so broad. His hair was a lighter color than Garth's, but his skin was tanned several shades darker, due, no doubt, to the sea voyage.

"Good evening, Mr. Stevens. I'm so happy to meet you."

Evers seemed speechless for a brief moment. "Not nearly so happy as I am in meeting you, Mrs. Stevens." His eyes twinkled as he took her hand, kissed it, and bowed low.

"Evers, you've grown since I last saw you." Garth held out his hand and, for a moment, Cara thought the younger brother would ignore it. But finally, he reached out and clasped his brother's hand.

"And do I perceive a slight softening in that terrible countenance?" Evers commented. He turned to Cara. "You must take the credit, ma'am; for I know when I last saw my brother, his face was one dark scowl."

The two men looked at each other, laughed, and finally clasped each other in comradeship.

"That's what I like to see," Aunt Lutie pronounced in a loud voice. "All the old quarrels forgotten. A fresh start. It does my heart good."

Jasper soon came in to announce supper, and Evers was quick to offer Cara his arm. "May I have the privilege of escorting my brother's beautiful wife?"

Cara looked at Garth and he nodded as he walked

to Aunt Lutie's side.

"Aunt Lutie, it looks as if we old folks will have to go in together. The young ones seem to have it all arranged."

Cara relaxed. The atmosphere seemed almost cordial at dinner with Evers, who was not at all like his brother. The conversation flowed while each course progressed. She was almost sorry to have the meal come to an end. She could have lingered a little longer, but with Aunt Lutie rising from the table, she had no recourse but to follow.

"I know you men would like to enjoy your cigars and brandy. Come, Cara, let's go into the drawing room. Those two can find their own way into the library."

Cara obediently obeyed Aunt Lutie.

"Now, tell me, dear," Aunt Lutie began. "Have you started thinking about clothes for the baby?"

"Yes, Aunt Lutie. But only thinking. I haven't had an opportunity to visit the shops yet, and I fear my sewing's not the best."

"I 'll be happy to take you to the right shops. And as for sewing, you'll have plenty of time for improving, with Garth away and not requiring a wife's attention.

"But tell me, since I gather you must have other interests, what do you enjoy?"

"I love to read...and paint in watercolors. And then there's music. But since I have no instrument, I've had no opportunity lately to practice," Cara lamented.

"Would you like to see my pianoforte? It's a Stein.

Perhaps you'll play it for me."

"Oh, no, I might disturb...someone. And besides, I brought no music with me."

"Nonsense." Aunt Lutie waved her hand, dismissing her protest. "You wouldn't disturb a soul. And I have some new music that has just arrived. Do you sing, too?"

"Yes. Some," she replied, and then modestly added, "but I'm not that good."

"Let me be the judge of that. Come, let's go into the music room."

Cara again followed Aunt Lutie. The moment she glimpsed the pianoforte, Cara became quite excited. Sitting down on the little gilt chair, she opened the lid of the instrument and quickly ran her fingers over the keys. The familiar tones reminded her of happier days, before her own pianoforte had been sold.

At first, her fingers were stiff and it took a little time to find the notes of an allemande, but with each phrase, the old dexterity began to return.

And when she began looking through the music on the pianoforte, she exclaimed, "Oh, Aunt Lutie, I see that you have some of the Scarlatti soprano cantatas. I sang one for the final graduation program at Miss Carey's School."

"Well, let me hear it, child."

The clear, lyric voice rose from the recitative to the beautiful, melodious aria—"*Solitudine avvenne, apriche celli' notte...*" As she accompanied herself on the keyboard, Cara was transported to another world.

"I vow I heard a nightingale sing."

Cara looked up. Evers was standing beside her.

"I'm sorry if I disturbed—"

"Disturbed?" he interrupted. "You mean entranced, don't you?"

Turning to his brother standing a bit farther away, he said, "What unmitigated luck to have a beautiful wife who can soothe you with her melodies. It would be your good fortune to have all the comforts..."

"Please... I..." Cara stood up, but Evers would not have it.

"No, you can't get away with a sample. We must have the full fare. Don't you agree, Aunt Lutie?"

"I most certainly do. That is, if she feels up to it."

"Sing something else for us, Cara," Evers requested.

Reluctantly, Cara looked through the sheets of music until she found another that she had sung— Scottish Songs by Beethoven. And although the music was not nearly so showy as the cantata, it gave emphasis to the rich, lower tones that she also possessed.

"Oh might I but my Patrick loved...he says we love too little prize, that gold too much bewitches. More blest the lark, tho' hard its doom when'er the winter rages, than birds, he says, of finer plume, that mope in golden cages..."

When she had finished, there was no sound in the room.

Evers, breaking the silence, said in a low voice, "I think, Cara, that you have the power to wreck men's souls—just as surely as the siren, the ships at sea."

Not understanding his reference, she turned a puzzled face to Garth. With a knowing smile, her husband replied to his brother, "Yes, one has to be careful not to be blinded by the golden hair, or succumb to the golden voice."

Aunt Lutie exclaimed impatiently, "Oh, you men! Always talking in riddles!"

Garth moved to Aunt Lutie's side. "As much as I would like to stay longer, I leave tomorrow, and must finish packing." And in a lower voice, he said, "You will take care of Cara while I'm gone?"

"Of course, Garth. The child will be well attended to. Evers and I will see to that."

"Come, Cara. It's time to go home."

"You must use my pianoforte regularly, Cara. Heaven knows it needs someone to play it besides an old crone who can't read half the notes."

"Thank you, Aunt Lutie—for everything. Goodbye, Evers."

"Goodbye, Cara." Turning to Garth, Evers said, "Take care, Brother, on your voyage." His eyes twinkled. "Remember, if anything happens to you, there'll be a long line of suitors for Cara, and I'll be the first in line."

Surprisingly, Garth laughed good-naturedly. "Then I'll be careful, Brother, that you don't inherit what is mine through default."

On the way home, Garth asked, "Did you like Aunt Lutie's pianoforte?"

"Yes, but..." She hesitated.

"But what, Cara? Let me hear your opinion."

"Well, there is a…a newer pianoforte—simpler, with more resonance. It's a Broadwood and…and even Mr. Beethoven is said to prefer it to all the others."

"And is that the kind you would wish to own—that is, if you ever owned one?"

"Yes." Her voice was soft and wistful.

Garth became pensive for the rest of the way home, and Cara, responsive to his mood, did not talk.

When they emerged from the carriage, Garth led her into the garden rather than going immediately into the house. He touched her cheek with his hand and she jumped, as if she had been struck.

"Cara mia," he whispered in the darkness. "I see that you are still afraid of me."

She shook her head. "No, I'm not afraid."

"Oh, but you are. And I understand why. Once, I hurt you when I should have been gentle. Yet, I would not hurt you now… At times, you have met me halfway, but then retreated farther from me. I have no wish for this wide breach to remain between us. When I'm away, I would like to picture you here—a loving wife, waiting patiently for her husband to return to her."

"Patiently?" Her voice became bitter. "Like your precious picture—without feeling, hanging on the wall only to come to life when you're around?"

"You seem to have no understanding of my feelings regarding the painting."

"And you seem to have no understanding of my

own feelings—to be reminded that, like the painting, I am only your possession."

"You made it clear one night that you were no man's possession."

"That was before you married me—before you threatened to send me to jail as a thief."

He groaned. "There was much that I should not have said, but you must understand. I had no choice. I could not let you go. I knew you were lost to me if I could not force you to marry me immediately."

"And I, too, had no choice," she replied.

"I see that there is to be no capitulation before I leave." He turned to stride up the walk to the door. "I hope you enjoy your revenge."

Cara remained, making no attempt to follow him. She had wanted to reach out and touch him and tell him that she was his, but her pride would not allow it. Not once had he ever said he loved her. Yet, he had told everyone that he was in love with the portrait, and he had made it plain to her how much his painting meant to him.

She bent to retrieve her fallen handkerchief and was aware of a whirring noise. When she tried to move, she realized her gown was caught on something. She jerked at it, but it would not come loose.

"Are you going to remain in the garden all night, Cara?"

"My gown. It's caught on something." She was still tugging at her dress when he reached her.

He leaned down to loosen it. "Oh, my God, Cara!"

He tore the dress to free her and swept her up after him, rushing to the steps and into the house.

"Did you have to tear my dress?"

"Yes." In his other hand, he held the culprit knife — the replica of the knife that had cut the painting, that had sliced the fruit at the breakfast table, and now had almost ended her life in the garden.

Looking at it, she remembered the whirring sound just as she bent over to retrieve her handkerchief. Realizing the close call, her knees became weak and she crumpled against her husband. Even then, she protested, "I...I'm all right. I won't faint."

Once they reached the house, he did not let her out of his sight, but remained in the bedroom. And instead of calling Molly to help her undress, Garth was the one to help her. But as she attempted to remove the strand of pearls, the clasp became caught in her dress.

"Oh, Garth, the pearls — you must get the lovely pearls free before they break," Cara cried.

He reached under the dress and upward to try to free the clasp from the material. But he was unsuccessful. And as she tried to get one arm out of the dress, she heard the rent of the delicate material.

"I think I have just ruined the dress," she lamented.

"Then, it doesn't matter if it's torn the rest of the way." So, with one swift motion, he completed the rent, with the dress falling from her body.

Later, he lay beside her, stroking the long golden hair that was now free of the rope of flowers that had been dropped on the floor beside the bed.

"Did you finish packing?" she inquired softly.

"No, but I 'll get up early in the morning to do so. " He hesitated and then added, "Cara, you must not come down to the wharf to see me off."

"But it will be a long time before —"

He kissed her on the lips. "We will say good-bye tonight."

"I don't even know the name of the ship you're sailing on."

"It's the *Northrop*, and it sails for Liverpool as soon as the tide is out. Now hush your chatter and save your voice for singing, my little witch. I need only your lips tonight."

He was gentle and she did not protest his hands upon her body. She only protested his bending her will to his...and that he seemed to have dismissed the fact that someone was trying to kill her.

Chapter 22

*T*he place beside her was empty, and Cara felt its emptiness in her heart. Her handsome, frightening husband had left her. Yesterday, she would have been glad, but today… Ah, today she was not so sure.

When he returned in three months, she would be so unshapely that he would not want to look at her.

She had failed in her effort to get him to love her; for he had thwarted her at every turn. And what was worse, against her will she had fallen in love with him. For that, she could not forgive herself.

But the child…She wrestled with her conscience. Bart was dead. And because of that, Cara knew she would always be torn. She would have no peace until she proved her brother's murderer. And there were too many things pointing to her own husband.

If only she had escaped, never to see Garth Stevens again. But now, it was too late. Sighing, she pulled the bell rope for Molly.

The morning passed so slowly that Cara checked to make sure all the clocks had not stopped in a conspiracy. A terrible loneliness welled up within her.

Cara was just finishing her lunch when she heard a noisy clatter on the street. Then, Aunt Lutie's voice, complaining in shrill tones, reached her ears.

Cara rushed to the door and bounded down the steps. There stood Aunt Lutie, indignantly berating the man on the mule wagon.

"Don't you know that's an expensive instrument? I never intended for it to be treated like a piece of junk. Be careful, man, or I shall have your hide!"

The pianoforte was being lowered to the street.

"Oh, Aunt Lutie—not your beautiful Stein pianoforte!" Cara gasped.

"I'm only lending it to you until that husband of yours can order one for you. It isn't right for you not to have one. Besides, you may not know it, dear, but there's been a change in plans. Evers and I are moving in with you until Garth returns. Some foolishness about not wanting you left alone for a minute. I can't always understand that man, even though he's my own flesh and blood. I never understood his father, either, come to think of it. I guess it just runs in the family."

"Garth asked you? I didn't know, but I'm pleased, Aunt Lutie. I hope it's not too inconvenient for you."

"No more inconvenient than being waked up before dawn. I do wish Garth had thought of it last night instead of coming this morning when I was sleeping best."

The trunks arrived later, and the house was in turmoil as Aunt Lutie, used to giving orders, had all the servants on the run. By evening, however; with the arrival of Evers, who was now seeing to the warehouse and shipping, the house had settled down to its normal calm.

After a long day, Aunt Lutie retired early, leaving only Cara and Evers in the drawing room. As Evers leisurely finished his brandy, he looked at the painting and then at Cara.

"Which came first, Cara?" he asked. "You or the painting?"

"The painting. I was merely—" She stopped, determined not to let him know how she felt about the *Cara Mia*.

"Do I detect a hint of animosity toward it?" He smiled as he waited for her answer.

"No. It's just that I don't—" Again she stopped, feeling trapped.

"It's all there, isn't it? Is that what frightens you about it? Seeing your hair, your eyes—all of your features captured by an artist so long ago?" He continued. "You know, there are some in tribal Africa who won't let a man draw his own image, for fear he will draw out his soul from his body, and he will go to live in that image. You're not that superstitious, are you, Cara?"

"Of course not, Evers," she murmured indignantly.

"And in the West Indies, " he continued, "those who practice voodoo believe if they destroy a picture or stick pins in the heart of an image, that person will die.

"Strange about that—I've seen it happen on ships among the imported. When the person discovers he's been marked for death, he actually dies, without anyone laying a hand on him."

"Are you trying to scare me, Evers? If you are," she responded with a forced laugh, "you're certainly succeeding."

All at once, a mortified look crossed his face. "Cara, I'm truly sorry. Please forgive me if I disturbed you. I've been among men for so long...I didn't intend to frighten you or to be so morbid."

Cara got up to take a closer look at the painting, and she could dimly see where it had been repaired—right in the area of the heart.

"Evers," she said slowly, "if someone believed in voodoo and wanted to kill me—though I was not around...could he slash the picture and...and believe his work had been done?"

By this time, a very concerned Evers was standing beside her. He stared at her and then back to the painting to examine the repair more closely.

"Cara, it's only a coincidence. I could kick myself for bringing up the subject."

"No, Evers. It's not a coincidence. Someone has tried several times to kill me, even after the slashing of the painting."

"So that 's why Garth told Aunt Lutie not to let you out of her sight. I had wondered at such an exaggerated request, even knowing Garth's jealousy."

"But I haven't the slightest idea of who would want

to kill me, or why…"

"What a terrible time for Garth to leave! If you were my wife, I'd—" He stopped abruptly. "But forget everything I said tonight."

Cara nodded. "I think it's time to retire. So I'll say good night, Evers."

"Good night, Cara. Sleep well," he added with a tenderness to his voice.

That night the rains began, and there was no hope in going out for the next few days until it had subsided. But with Aunt Lutie and Evers in the house, patterns were soon established.

Not too long after dinner each evening, Aunt Lutie would retire, leaving Cara and Evers to remain awhile longer in either the drawing room or the library.

Evers had taken to speaking lightly of amusing things, and Cara was aware that he was deliberately avoiding any subject that might upset her.

Nevertheless, she felt quite comfortable with him— more so than with Garth. Perhaps it was because Evers was nearer her own age.

After that first night, when she had lain awake for hours because of the troubling conversation about the painting, she had begun to sleep better—even dismissing the implications. Evers was probably right, just a coincidence in all the happenings.

When Aunt Lutie had been in the house for little more than a week, Cara heard her voice in the hall on an early sunny morning.

The woman, fully dressed, swept into the room. "Up, my pet! Today is the day to go shopping, and we need to get an early start. I do hate it so when the shops get crowded with riffraff later in the day."

Aunt Lutie walked over to the bell pull. "We mustn't waste the cool morning."

Amused, Cara sat up in bed. She was eager to go to the shops, so she did not protest. Yet, by the time she had eaten breakfast and dressed, it was still early and Cara wondered if the shops had even opened. But Aunt Lutie prevailed and when the two walked out of the town house, Henry was ready with the landau, taking them down the main thoroughfare.

The vendors were also out early, hawking their wares, each giving the impression that his were the best buys of the day.

"She crab! Get yo' she crabs!"

"Swimpy! Raw swimpy!"

A young boy sang out, dancing in rhythm to his chant. "Straw-ber-ry! Fresh straw-ber-ry! Mighty fine — straight frum de vine!"

"Stop here, Henry, in the shade," Aunt Lutie ordered. "We'll be gone for some time. So unhitch the horses and water them, and then you can see to some refreshments for yourself." She reached into her purse and handed him a silver piece.

"Thank you, ma'am."

"Come, Cara, I want you to see Mister Goodin's shop first. He's just gotten in a new shipment and we should be able to find some appropriate material."

Cara was fascinated by the sights and smells of the street, and she lagged behind Aunt Lutie as the purposeful woman marched down the cobblestones to Mister Goodin's shop.

"Mrs. Cowper, how nice to see you, ma'am." The man behind the counter came forward to greet them.

"Mister Goodin—my nephew's wife, Mrs. Garth Stevens. She needs materials for a layette, and I told her that you have some of the finest. So don't try to palm off any old thing you happen to have left from the previous shipment. We want to see your best."

"How do you do, Mrs. Stevens? Mrs. Cowper *always* recognizes the best. I could never deceive her. And I do have some mighty fine material. Just a moment, and I'll go and fetch it." In a low voice, he confessed, "I don't always put my prime goods on display."

Cara smiled. She had an idea that he said the same thing to each of his regular customers to make her feel special. She could also see how pleased Aunt Lutie was with the attention. Fascinated by the shelves of goods, Cara wandered around the shop while Mister Goodin was busy in the back of his shop.

The little bell on the door rang as another customer entered. Suddenly a voice called out, "Ginny! Ginny Carter!"

Startled, Cara looked up. As the young woman approached her, she recognized her best friend from school– Elsine.

With delight, Cara said, "Elsine, is it really you? I can't belive it! What are your doing here in Charleston?"

"I'm married now," Elsine replied, blushing. "We moved here just a few weeks ago."

"I'm so happy for you. Whom did you marry? And where do you live?"

"His name is Anthony Lyle and he's just inherited his uncle's plantation. It's upriver, about five miles from here. It's called Weedon Hall. Perhaps you've heard of it? But tell me about *you*."

"Well," Cara hesitated. "I'm married, too — to Garth Stevens, But he calls me 'Cara' and not 'Ginny.' "

"How romantic!"

They stared at each other and then began laughing; for they both recognized the barely perceptible signs of impending motherhood.

"Did you say your husband is the famous Garth Stevens? The elusive one that all the mamas around here wanted for their daughters? I must say, he's quite the most handsome man around, except for my own husband."

"Do you know him?" Cara asked in surprise.

"Not really. I had only heard about him. But this morning as we rode into town, my husband pointed him out to me. But he was going so fast on his horse that I didn't get a really good look. Yet, even a quick glimpse was enough for me to see he is one handsome man! Tell me, Ginny, I mean, Cara — how did you meet him?"

"I...I fell from my horse and he rescued me. But Elsine, your husband must be mistaken," Cara said, frowning. "He sailed on the *Northrop* for Liverpool over a week ago."

"Well, then, we couldn't possibly have seen him. But perhaps I misunderstood—although I feel sure that was the name Anthony mentioned."

Aunt Lutie called to Cara and as she said good-bye to Elsine, she added, "Come to see me if you can. Right now I'm staying in town until the baby comes. I'm in the three-story white house on East Bay Street."

"We're staying in town, too. Anthony has taken a house on Church Street for the next few months. I'll come visit you soon."

When Cara and Aunt Lutie returned from their long day of shopping, Calhoun Wilkes was sitting in the drawing room.

"I came to see how Cara was faring, with her husband away," he said to Aunt Lutie, "but if you're taking her in tow, then I know there's nothing to worry about." He leaned over to kiss his aunt on the forehead with a noisy smack.

"Oh, you flirty boy! Save your kisses for someone who appreciates them." She pretended to be offended.

"But I thought you appreciated them, Aunt Lutie," he teased.

"Not half so much as some flighty young girl. I declare, Calhoun, if you don't make up your mind and marry soon, you're going to be a toothless old bachelor, and no pretty girl will look at you twice."

He glanced at Cara. "I did have someone in mind, But, as usual, Garth wouldn't let me have her."

Cara laughed. "I'm so glad to see you. You always make me laugh."

He feigned a hurt look. "You see, dear aunt,—when I'm serious, everyone laughs."

"Would you like something to drink, Calhoun?" Cara asked. "Aunt Lutie and I were just going to have some tea. Or would you prefer something stronger? Garth has some good brandy…"

"Then, brandy, by all means."

When the older woman left the room to direct Russell with the packages, Cara remained with Calhoun, seeing to his brandy.

On impulse, she said, "Will you stay for supper, Calhoun? Evers should be back here soon and—"

"Evers?" he said in surprise. "When did he get back?"

"A few days before Garth left. He and Aunt Lutie are staying with me until Garth returns. You will remain for supper, won't you?"

"How can I refuse when asked so prettily?" He bowed low. "Madam, I am at your command."

"At whose command?" Evers asked, standing in the doorway.

"So the prodigal brother returns," Calhoun said. He reached out and shook Evers' hand, as he assessed the young man. "I must say you've changed since I last saw you. The sea air seems to have done you good."

As the two became reacquainted after such a long time apart, Cara said, "If you two will excuse me, I"ll get ready for supper."

The evening was a light, cordial one. After supper, Cara, at Evers' insistence, played the pianoforte and sang. The two men vied with each other to turn the pages of the music, and a contented Aunt Lutie listened, while her busy fingers made intricate stitches on the soft material she had purchased earlier.

Finally, Cara closed the lid and stood up. "I do not wish to bore you any further."

"Never enough," Evers complained. "She stops too soon."

"Better than not stopping soon enough," Cara answered, her amethyst eyes twinkling.

"Well, if there's to be no further entertainment, then I must be on my way," Calhoun said. "It's been a delightful evening, Family, and I hope we can get together again soon.

" Good night, my lovely cousin, and take care. Good night, my favorite aunt."

Evers saw him to the door. "You're not going to try to make it back to the plantation tonight, are you, Cal?"

"No, Evers. I'm staying in town."

"At the Planter's Hotel?"

"No…with a friend."

They both laughed.

Chapter 23

*T*he summer social season was now at its height. Aunt Lutie and Cara had already been squired by Evers and Calhoun to several different supper parties and one St. Cecilia concert by a French immigrant from Barbados. Cara's pregnancy had been well disguised, but she still hesitated each time.

"Do you think I should go, Aunt Lutie—without my husband, and especially in my condition?"

"Pshaw, child! Don't be so prim. No one can talk about you while I'm your chaperone and, after all, Evers and Calhoun are family. You'll be confined all too soon. So we'll make the most of it while we can."

"If you think it's all right." Cara was still uncertain.

"Of course it is. We're not so puritan as those New Englanders. We at least know where babies come from, and don't consider it a sin unless the girl can't get the man to marry her before the baby arrives."

"But I don't want Evers or Calhoun to feel put upon. They should be escorting eligible young ladies to parties, instead of—"

"Let that be your least worry, Cara." Aunt Lutie chuckled. "Those two boys see the advantages of the situation all too well, when the mamas of those eligible young ladies become too insistent. So it works both ways. We protect them and they escort us."

"Who are you protecting, Aunt Lutie?" Evers asked, entering the drawing room in his elegant evening clothes.

"Those that need it," Aunt Lutie replied dryly.

Evers looked first at Cara and then to Aunt Lutie. "It looks as if I'll be busy tonight protecting two beautiful ladies from all the gentlemen."

"Oh, hush your flattery, Evers Stevens, and see if the carriage is ready." Aunt Lutie smoothed her flounce of lace around her generous bosom.

"I hear the Widower Devereau will be at the party tonight. He's looking around for his next wife, and everybody knows that he was sweet on you at one time." Evers had a teasing look in his eyes. "Are you going to lead him on tonight, Aunt Lutie?"

"Louis Devereau is a fool—and you know I wouldn't marry a fool at my age. He'll just have to keep looking until he finds some idiot who'll say yes to him. It won't be me," she snapped.

"You'll break his heart tonight, poor man." With mock sympathy, Evers went to see to the carriage.

Calhoun arrived and the four left in a carefree mood. The carriage, driven by Henry, made its way to Meeting Road, on to King Street, and finally to the last street at the end of town.

"They might as well live in the country. I declare, I don't see why the Wilkinsons would build so far away from things," Aunt Lutie commented.

"There are no more building sites in the heart of town. This is the only way the town can grow."

"They could have bought a house that was already built," Aunt Lutie countered.

"I understand there's a house up for sale on Tradd Street," Cara joined in.

"Yes," said Calhoun. "I looked at it yesterday, thinking I might buy it."

"You, Cal? Are you getting married? Who's the lucky girl?" asked Cara.

"No—no girl involved. I just think it would be to my advantage to have a house in town where I can entertain."

"Entertain?" Evers laughed. "What kind of entertaining would you do without a wife?"

Calhoun grew angry at Evers' insinuation. "Your brother had a town house long before he had a wife."

Suddenly there was an awkward silence, when no one spoke. Cara did not like to be reminded of Garth's life before she met him. She was well aware, because of Sonia, of his former habits.

"Here we are," a relieved Aunt Lutie said. "My, look at all the lights. It's a lovely place," she conceded, "even if it is too far out."

They entered the house, once more at ease with each other.

Aunt Lutie immediately greeted their hostess."Katie Wilkinson, I love your house. But why did you build it in this wilderness?"

"Lutie Cowper," she replied, "that's called progress. Now, introduce me to your family."

"My niece, Cara Stevens. She's married to Garth, you know, but he's in London. And these are my two nephews, Calhoun Wilkes and Evers Stevens.

"Evers has recently gotten home from sea, and Calhoun's busy with his merchant ships and his river plantation. Both are mighty eligible bachelors, I might add."

Katie Wilkinson was delighted. "I have some lovely girls for you two to meet."

Before they had left their hostess's side, an elderly, somewhat portly man descended upon them. "Lutie, I knew that voice the moment I heard it."

"Louis! Louis Devereau! What are you doing in town?" Aunt Lutie acted as if it were a great surprise to see him.

He took her by the arm, and Cara was left with Evers and Calhoun.

"There's no need for both of you to stay with me," Cara stated. "Why don't you draw straws? The loser can stay with me and the winner can flirt with all the pretty young girls."

"You're wrong, Cara. The winner would stay with you," Evers replied.

"Spoken like a true gallant, Brother-in-law," Cara responded in kind.

The three were soon surrounded by young people, all talking at once. Cara's eyes lit up when she saw Elsine walking toward her.

"Ginny, I want you to come and meet my husband." She took Cara's hand and led her away from the group.

"This is my husband, Anthony," Elsine said proudly, love showing in her eyes.

"Anthony, I want you to meet my dearest friend from school, Ginny Carter. She's married to Garth Stevens, and I guess I'll have to get used to calling her Cara. That's what her husband calls her."

"Are you related to Bart Carter?" the man asked.

Garth's admonition—never to reveal her true name—caused her to hesitate. But her past was already compromised by her friendship with Elsine, so she saw little harm in admitting it.

"Yes. He was my brother."

"Was?" he repeated, "Do you mean...?"

"He's dead," Cara said with little emotion in her voice.

"I'm so sorry. I didn't know."

Suddenly with Calhoun appearing at Cara's side she made the introductions.

"This is my husband's cousin, Calhoun Wilkes—Elsine and Anthony Lyle."

Calhoun shook the proffered hand.

"Mr. Lyle has just inherited Weedon Hall," Cara prompted. "As one plantation owner to another, I'm sure you have much to talk about."

She smiled vaguely at them and wandered away.

Evers had been cornered by one of the fathers, and Cara saw the look on his face as he was led toward the plain daughter, sitting with her mother.

As the evening progressed, with no breeze stirring, Cara began to feel the heat, made worse by the overwhelming, sickening sweet perfume of tuberoses on every table. So, at the first chance, Cara walked toward the open door to seek relief.

"Cara, are you all right?" Again, Calhoun was at her side.

"I feel terrible, Cal. I only wish I could go home now."

He helped her to a bench on the piazza and went to find Aunt Lutie.

"Oh, dear! Calhoun says you're feeling ill, Cara, and I told Henry not to come back for at least another hour." Aunt Lutie was clearly disturbed.

"I have my phaeton here," Louis Devereau offered. "There's only room for two, but perhaps one of your nephews could take her home in it, and I can ride with you later to pick it up."

Aunt Lutie thought for a moment. "That does seem to be the best solution. You'll take good care of her, won't you, Cal, and see that one of the servants goes for Dr. Blondeau as soon as you get home?"

"Of course, Aunt Lutie."

Louis went to fetch his horses and the phaeton, and soon Cara was sitting beside Calhoun on the way back to the town house.

"I'm sorry that you had to leave the party because of me, Cal."

"It's all right, Cara. I promised Garth I would look after you. Besides, the party was getting to be quite boring."

They had gone only a mile or so when Calhoun asked, "Are you finally getting your memory back, Cara?"

"Why do you ask?"

"I thought I heard you tell Anthony Lyle that Bart Carter was your brother."

Cara hesitated. "Yes. At least I'm beginning to remember some things from my past. Did you know him, Calhoun?"

"Only casually. We played cards together sometimes."

"Tell me, do you know how he died? When was the last time you saw him?"

"It was that night at the Planter's Hotel...when he and Garth had the fight..."

Cara gasped and Calhoun quickly reassured her. "I didn't mean to give the impression that it was Garth—" He stopped , staring at the road ahead.

The glow of the moon picked out the white shirt of a man running across the road to the shelter of a palmetto tree, while another man shifted his position behind one of the rocks jutting out near the road .

Startled to see the two behaving so suspiciously, Cara whispered, ""Cal, those men..."

Calhoun evidently saw them as well, but too late.

He didn't have enough time to turn the horses around.

"Cara, remain quiet, but hold on tight for a sudden dash."

Cal held the reins tensely, not giving the horses their head until they were almost upon the men. Then, with an awful shout, he stood up and slapped the horses into a frenzied gallop. They shot past the two men, leaving them cursing in the dust.

Cal had remained standing, but suddenly blood spurted from his arm. He sat down in surprise, at first not realizing that he had been hit and almost losing the reins. Without knowing what had happened, Cara grabbed the reins.

Then she saw his arm. "You're hurt, Cal!"

He looked down at the blood seeping through his sleeve. "Hush, beautiful one. It's not a serious wound. I'll live."

When Cara entered the town house, with her dress stained in Calhoun's blood, Molly, certain that her mistress was dying, became hysterical. She ran from the town house and didn't stop until she reached Dr. Blondeau's house several blocks away.

Russell woke up all the servants and sent Henry immediately to pick up Aunt Lutie and Evers.

By the time the partygoers arrived home, with Louis Devereau, Dr. Blondeau had treated both patients and even calmed Molly. Much to the relief of everyone, Cal's wound was minor.

"I should have been with them," Evers said over and

over. "I was supposed to be protecting Cara."

"I'm more at fault than you are, Evers," Aunt Lutie insisted. "I should not have sent Henry back. From now on, we will all stick together."

Louis Devereau returned the next day to show them the knife he had found lodged in his phaeton, before taking the weapon on to the sheriff's office.

Once again, Cara recognized its familiar shape. Only this one had a notch on the handle. How many more knives would appear, seeking to do damage before someone was apprehended?

The notch worried her. Had Garth's knife he had used at the breakfast table not had a notch on it, also?

Could it possibly be Garth's knife? But no. That was impossible. Her husband was in London, far away....

Chapter 24

Cara's days fell into a pattern, and she became quite content, despite the troubling events that had occurred earlier. She and Elsine visited occasionally, comparing their sewing as well as their sizes.

Under the tutelage of Aunt Lutie, Cara's sewing became passable, and she took pride in the number of tiny garments she had completed. And since Aunt Lutie had taken over making the more complicated clothes—little coats and bonnets— she no longer saw the need of engaging Miss Barnes, the dressmaker.

Dr. Blondeau visited regularly and he seemed pleased with her good health.

Each week, Calhoun came to visit, and although she was now large with child, she still enjoyed the teasing rivalry between Evers and his cousin over who would hand her the scissors or fetch her footstool.

And then came that awful day in September, shortly before Garth was due to arrive home.

Evers walked slowly into the drawing room, and his

face showed a terrible sadness as he said, "Cara, put down your sewing."

She laid aside the garment she had been working on and, bewildered at his request, looked up at her brother-in-law. "What is it?"

He sat beside her on the sofa and took her hand in his. "The *Northrop*..." He started again, "The *Northrop* has been lost at sea. There are no survivors."

Cara pulled her hand away. "No! I don't believe you! It can't be true!"

"But it is, Cara." Evers' voice broke. "Sailors from the *Caddington* found part of the wreckage. The ship never got to Liverpool."

The baby kicked, as if in anger at the news, and Cara fainted against Evers.

When Cara came to, she was in bed. Dr. Blondeau, with sad eyes, was bending over her. "I'm so sorry," he murmured.

"So it's true," she said, realizing that her tall, handsome, frightening husband would never come home to her or the child.

Aunt Lutie and the servants tiptoed in and out of her room, bringing nourishment and comfort to her, but she refused both.

The hours passed, with Cara in a suspended state— neither in tune with reality, nor entirely in a dream world.

"You must think of the child, Cara. Garth would not want you to grieve so; for it hurts the baby," Aunt Lutie reminded her.

Cara could still hear his angry words when he had hung the painting in the drawing room. "I expect you to take care of my possessions, Cara—my painting—my child…"

She knew that she must obey him, even in death.

She called for food, and then a bath. Dressing in the flowing pink dressing gown that she had found in one of the shops when she and Aunt Lutie had last gone shopping, she left her bedroom. Her hair hung down her back in curling strands of gold, streaked with moon glow.

Reaching the salon, she stood before the painting—the *Cara Mia*—and for the first time she was able to look at the painting with no revulsion.

Hardly able to tell which was the canvas, which the living flesh, Evers stood spellbound in the doorway.

He came to her then, his boyish face serious and concerned. "I'm glad to see that you're up, Cara."

"It wasn't good for the child," she replied, "to give in to grief. But Evers, what am I to do?"

The tears spilled from the sad, amethyst eyes, and in his desire to comfort her, he reached out to her.

"I'll always take care of you, beautiful Cara," he murmured in an anguished whisper.

She turned and faced the painting again, pretending that she had not heard him; for she knew that the words had slipped out, and he would be embarassed when he realized what he had said.

Nevertheless, each day Evers took on more responsibility, and anyone coming into the house would not have guessed that he was merely the brother-in-law, and not her husband.

He saw to financial matters, to the running of the house, with Aunt Lutie's help. He changed from a boy to a man, becoming the head of the family. But at the same time, the bantering rivalry between Evers and Calhoun ceased, to be replaced by a growing antagonism. And Aunt Lutie, noticing it, was helpless to do anything about it.

Her only recourse was to warn Cara and give her motherly advice.

"Cara, I've outlived three husbands, each one a fine man," Aunt Lutie confided. "But I can never forget my first one — my true love. When he died, I didn't want to go on living, but as time went by, I became lonely. I felt that he would want me to live enough for the both of us. So I fit together the pieces and built my life again; yet never forgetting him.

"I know that Garth would wish you to do the same, although it's far too early to be decently talking about it. But I don't think you're aware of what's happening, so a word of warning: Evers is in love with you and so is Calhoun."

Cara looked at Aunt Lutie in amazement.

"Calhoun's mother was a Stevens, you know. Both he and Evers have what I call the 'Stevens temper.' It might not be so apparent as it was in Garth. He never made any attempt to hide it, but I have seen both Calhoun and Evers when they're crossed, and it's not pretty to watch."

"You're frightening me, Aunt Lutie."

"Well, I believe that forewarned is forearmed. Remember this warning when the proper time comes."

Cara was not sure that she had understood. She looked down, noting her ripe, round body and concluding that Aunt Lutie had been mistaken. No man could be in love with her during this time.

September passed slowly. October, with its lovely cool days, brought some relief to Cara, but she was still as heavy in heart as she was with child.

Since she could not be seen in public, or ride over the rough streets in the landau, Dr. Blondeau encouraged her to engage in mild exercise with strolls in the garden. But by the end of October, when the first killing frost arrived, even that was denied her.

So the visit one day from Calhoun was a welcome one. He rubbed his hands before the fire and stamped his feet on the hearth rug.

"Did you ride all the way from the river plantation?" Cara asked.

"Yes. Stupid of me. I should have come yesterday, when it was warmer."

"Let me get you some hot cider," Cara offered.

"No. Don't get up. I'll ring for Russell." He turned back to Cara. "It won't be long now, will it?"

"Perhaps another month. I know it's not proper to be discussing my confinement, but since it's so obvious and since I consider you part of the family…"

His eyes softened as he spoke to her. "I'm glad that you recognize that I'm part of the family, Cara. So I 'll repeat what I said to you months ago. If you ever consider changing abodes, the wisteria blooms sweeter; the moss hangs lower, and the welcome is always there…"

"Thank you, Calhoun. You're very kind."

"I don't mean to be kind, Cara."

"I…I do not know how Garth has disposed of his property, or…or whether the baby — "

At that moment, Russell entered and Cara did not continue.

"Mister Calhoun would like some hot cider, Russell. He's just ridden into town from the plantation."

"It's a mighty cold day, Mister Calhoun. Don't know when I've ever seen a colder Hallow's Eve. I'll get that cider for you. And would you like anything, Miss Cara?"

"I think I'd like some cider, too, Russell. Thank you."

When Russell had gone, Cal asked, "Where is Aunt Lutie?"

"She's at her own house, giving instructions to the servants. Evers took her. I feel so guilty that she has had to remain here with me, but she never complains."

"She feels needed, and that's very important to her. I've never seen her look so young. And the last time I saw her, she even stepped higher when she walked."

Evers and Aunt Lutie arrived at the same time that Russell brought in the two mugs of cider. Before Cara had a chance to take a sip, Evers walked over and, in a familiar gesture, he begged the mug from her. "Let me drink of yon mug; for I'm fair famished with cold." He drank several gulps of the hot liquid before handing it back to Cara.

"Dear brother, if I should ever want to poison thee, I should but poison mine own cup," she replied playfully, and they both burst into laughter.

The scene was not lost on Calhoun. An angry look crossed his face as he turned toward the fire.

Chapter 25

$\mathcal{F}$or the next week, discomfort and heaviness were with Cara, and so by the time the pains began, she was actually glad.

When she pulled the bell rope for Molly that morning, the servant appeared as if she had already been waiting outside the door.

"Molly, I think we'll have to send word for Dr. Blondeau..."

"Oh, Miss Cara, have the pains already started?"

"Yes. Earlier this morning. But I didn't want to get anyone up so early."

"Babies don't care about other folks, or the time of day. When they're ready to come, they're ready."

In a few moments, the entire household was in a state of excitement.

"But you can't go into her bedroom, Evers." Aunt Lutie's voice carried up the hall.

"I can and I will. You forget, Aunt Lutie, I'm the head of this house now."

"But you're not the father of the baby."

There was a pause, then Evers replied, "Soon that won't matter."

When Evers knocked on the door, Molly opened it.

"Cara," he said softly, taking her hand. She smiled up at him and then tightly grasped his hand as another pain bore down upon her. He stayed by her side until Dr. Blondeau arrived.

"I won't be far away, Cara," he said before he was dismissed from the room. And she could hear him pacing up and down in the corridor.

Aunt Lutie, hovering near the door, said, "Please do your pacing elsewhere, Evers, or go to the library and finish that scuppernong wine. You're in the way up here. It will take hours for this baby to get here, and Dr. Blondeau will have three patients on his hands instead of the two he's supposed to be looking after, if you don't settle down."

"She's right, Mr. Stevens," Dr. Blondeau said, as he emerged from the bedroom. "It will be hours yet, so we'll both be better off downstairs, while Miss Lutie takes a turn sitting with her."

Reluctantly, Evers left.

"I've never seen an uncle so upset at the birth of his kin," Aunt Lutie said, coming to sit beside Cara. "I declare, he's taking it as hard as any father."

"He's had to put up with so much these past months, Aunt Lutie," Cara replied before another pain caused her to gasp.

Calmly wiping Cara's forehead after each spasm,

Aunt Lutie kept up a casual conversation to pass the time.

"I just hope Evers will last through the day. I told him to drink some of that scuppernong wine to dull his senses." Aunt Lutie gazed at Cara in sympathy. "I wish there was something to dull your pain a little, too, my dear. But this travail seems to be the lot of mothers."

"I...I only wish that Garth..."

"We all feel that way, Cara. It's hard enough to bring a child into the world as it is, but when the father—"

Aunt Lutie turned her head away for a moment. "But we're your family now, and we'll always take care of you and Garth's child."

The day aged slowly, from morning to afternoon. The afternoon grew old and passed into evening, and still the baby had not made its appearance.

Molly, Aunt Lutie, and Dr. Blondeau had all taken turns sitting with Cara, until Dr. Blondeau took over.

"Bear down, Cara," Dr. Blondeau insisted at last. "It won't be much longer now."

Cara bit hard on her parched lips, trying to suppress the scream that was waiting in her throat. Molly wiped the residue of moisture from her brow, while Aunt Lutie, never too religious, frowned in concentration, trying to remember the words of a prayer.

At last, with one last rending of her body, the new life separated from Cara's own, and when her sharp cry pierced the room, she sank back on the pillows in relief—not knowing whether the sound had come from her own lips or that of her child's.

"It's a girl, Cara," Dr. Blondeau said. "You have a fine, beautiful little girl."

"I think I'll go down for a glass of that scuppernong wine—that is, if Evers hasn't drunk it all," a shaky Aunt Lutie said.

It was sometime later that Evers and Calhoun, who had both been waiting downstairs, came into the room, with Aunt Lutie at their side.

"Only for a moment," Dr. Blondeau ordered. "She's exhausted."

Cara, her face pale and weary, proudly displayed her tiny, golden-haired daughter in her arms.

"She's beautiful," Evers whispered in awe.

"Yes, she is," Calhoun agreed, but he was staring into Cara's amethyst eyes.

"What are you going to name her?" Evers asked.

"Carina," the young mother answered. "Garth would have liked that…"

As each day followed another, with Cara's total concern centered on caring for her baby, she did not realize that Cal had not returned for a visit since the night of Carina's birth. It was only when Aunt Lutie said, "I wonder where Calhoun could be. He seems to have disappeared," that she began to wonder, also, about his absence.

Evers, joining in the conversation, remarked, "You're not the only one, Aunt Lutie. They were asking about him at the Exchange this morning. He hasn't been seen in town, and I understand that he isn't at his plantation either."

"Do you think something has happened to him?" a suddenly worried Cara asked.

Aware that Cara did not look well, Evers was quick to answer, "There's nothing to be alarmed about, I'm sure. He's probably taken a trip somewhere, and neglected to tell anyone. He'll be popping up soon with a likely story to relate of his adventuresome escapade."

Cara looked relieved, but Aunt Lutie and Evers glanced anxiously at each other, concerned, not only for Calhoun, but for Cara's health.

Dr. Blondeau was also concerned and a wet nurse for Carina was engaged, although she protested.

"Your recovery is slow, Cara, and the baby is taking what little strength you have," Dr. Blondeau admonished. "You must allow me to decide what's best for you."

"But I hardly get to be with her! Molly won't let me lift a finger and Aunt Lutie is just as bad. I'll never see my baby if I don't even nurse her."

"No one is trying to take her from you, Cara. You can care for her completely after you're well and strong. But you need to rest for the next several weeks, without being waked up at night."

Dr. Blondeau proved to be a wise man. As soon as Cara began to get a good night's sleep, without being awakened by a hungry Carina, a healthy glow chased away the pallor of the previous weeks.

The slim, comely Cara looked even more beautiful in mourning. The black shawl around her shoulders—the outward symbol of her grief—only accented the fair, flawless complexion and the pale gold hair that she wore woven into a plait around her proud head.

The Widow Stevens...It was hard to reconcile herself to that title. It was a term for someone old and gray—an aged woman, sitting in a straight chair— a grandmother peering myopically at her needlework, while her grandchildren played by the hearth.

But Margaret McAlistair was a widow, too, and although not so young as Cara, still she was not of sufficient age to let life pass her by. How had she managed through those first long, grief-stricken months?

Aware of Russell, the houseman, standing before her, Cara said, "What is it, Russell?"

"The Widow McAlistair is here to see you, ma'am."

"Show her in, Russell."

Cara smiled inwardly. It seemed that she still possessed that witchlike quality of conjuring up someone in her mind, only to have that person appear. It had happened more than once—a feeling—a fleeting thought—and that person became flesh and blood before her eyes.

"Mrs. McAlistair, how good it is to see you." Cara came forward to greet her plantation neighbor.

"Call me Margaret, if you will. It seems that we are more closely bound together than ever before."

Cara nodded and replied, "And you must call me Cara." She immediately asked, "Will you have some refreshment? I was just ready to put my sewing aside for tea."

"Yes, thank you. It's been a rather tiring trip into town, and I didn't stop on the way."

"Will you have tea or chocolate?"

"Tea, please."

Seeing the dark circles under Margaret's eyes, Cara asked, "Have you been well, I hope?"

"I *did* suffer a little ague," she confessed. "This summer I stayed at Sussex Hall, you know. There was so much to do. The rice birds were unusually plaguesome, but even then, we managed to get a good harvest."

As Cara poured the tea from the old silver teapot that had been in Garth's family for generations, Margaret was silent. But once she held the delicate cup in her hands, she said, "I 'm so sorry about Garth."

The pain showed in Cara's face. "Margaret, how...how could you stand it when... when your husband..." The tears sprang to her eyes.

"Nothing helped at first," a sympathetic Margaret admitted. "Only time can dull the ache." But then Margaret's voice changed. "Cara, are you absolutely certain that Garth was on the *Northrop*? Could he have sailed on another ship?"

"Thank you for attempting to give me hope, Margaret. But I'm certain that he was on the *Northrop*."

"At least you have something to remember him by—his child."

Cara's face brightened. "Would you like to see her, Margaret? That is, if you don't mind walking up the stairs?"

"I would love to see her."

Together the two left the sitting room and walked up to the third floor nursery.

The baby was awake. Cara picked her up from the cradle to show her proudly to her visitor.

Margaret looked at the baby and back to Cara. "She's quite beautiful. I know Garth would have been so proud of his daughter. What have you named her?"

"Carina."

"I'm very envious, you know. I had always hoped to have children…"

"It's not too late, Margaret. You're still young."

Abruptly Margaret said, "I must be going. My friends are expecting me."

"If you have a chance, come back to see us. Aunt Lutie will be sorry to have missed you."

Chapter 26

*O*n the next morning when Cara awoke, she slowly opened her eyes and looked around, noting the familiar furnishings of her bedroom—the same armoire; the same silk wallpaper on the walls. She seemed almost surprised that nothing had changed.

Her dream had been so vivid, and she sat up, trying to recall it, before it vanished. She shivered as she remembered the feeling, the dark surroundings in an old palazzo, with the embroidered tapestry, the high-backed blue velvet chair, and the familiar smell of pigments, as an artist ground his colors.

Garth had been in her dream, too, but he had looked vastly different, standing and watching her from the shadows.

Had she longed for Garth so much that she had begun dreaming about him? Yes, that must be it. But why were they in a different setting, so foreign from Mosshaven? Cara, determined to dismiss the troubling dream, climbed out of bed to face another day.

The baby was now six weeks old. With her bright golden hair and amethyst eyes, she was becoming more like Cara every day.

"My child will be so spoiled," Cara commented. "She has only to utter a sound and someone picks her up…and Evers is the worst one."

"That little Carina," Aunt Lutie said, chuckling. "I've never seen such a tiny baby wrap a man around her finger like that. Most men don't pay any attention to little girls. In fact, they have no idea what to do with them. But that baby already knows how to snuggle her way into a man's heart. She's going to be a little Charleston heartbreaker, mark my words."

Cara looked down at her sleeping child as the Christmas Eve chimes of Saint Michael's filled the air.

"Do you think every mother feels the same when she watches her baby sleeping? I want so much for Carina — everything that is fine and good…"

"Yes, Cara. I expect even the Virgin Mary must have felt the same way on that first Christmas Day when she looked down at *her* sleeping child."

"But do you think she had any idea what lay ahead — the pain and suffering? I don't think I could bear it if something terrible were to happen to little Carina."

"There, child. You're thinking too much. It addles the brain, you know, to be too serious. Besides, can't you feel the gaiety in the air?"

Aunt Lutie, as if suddenly remembering the Christmas feast, got up from the sofa. "I'd better see how

Flora is coming along with that roast goose. And I do hope that Calhoun will finally appear in time for the family gathering. He hasn't missed a single Christmas Eve dinner with me for the last ten years, and he'd better not start now!"

"When do we open the presents?" a voice boomed from the hall. Calhoun stood with his arms loaded with presents.

Cara rushed to greet him. "Cal, where have you been? We've been so worried about you."

"Business kept me away. Did you miss me?"

"You know we did, Cal—Evers, Aunt Lutie..."

"And what about you, Cara?" he pressed, looking at her carefully.

"Of course I missed you," she said hurriedly, and then smiled. "Come into the sitting room and see the baby. Then, I'll help you take your packages to the upstairs drawing room... That's where we have the tree. You should see it with the candles all over it... I'm glad the Germans brought their custom with them. I love the idea of a bright, flaming Christmas tree..."

She did not know why she was chattering so, or why she suddenly felt uncomfortable in Calhoun's presence.

Carina's cry greeted her as the baby awoke, wet and hungry. Aunt Lutie appeared and, seeing Calhoun, she began voicing her indignation at his staying away so long.

By the time Molly came in to take the baby back to

the nursery, Aunt Lutie had softened her reproach to her nephew, and Evers, hearing the noise, joined them.

"Have you explained your absence to Aunt Lutie's satisfaction, Cal?" he asked.

"I hope so, Evers. Can't have my favorite aunt angry at me, you know."

After the packages had been put under the Christmas tree, the family group went into the dining room.

Flora and Zennia had taken special pains with the Christmas Eve dinner. Roast goose, plum pudding, rice, cranberry jelly, and scuppernong wine vied with the pleasant conversation. A momentary sadness — that she had not been able to spend one Christmas Eve with Garth — was forcibly dispelled.

When the dinner was over, the family went into the drawing room, where Evers lit the candles on the tree. The room glowed with its light.

But then a clatter drifted up from the street and Aunt Lutie, hearing it, said, "Good heavens! What is that noise? Can't a family enjoy a quiet celebration without being disturbed?"

"Beg your pardon, Miss Cara. There's a man at the door. Says he has a Christmas present for you," Russell apologized.

"For me? But I'm not expecting anything to be delivered."

"I'll go and see what it is," Evers offered.

There was a shuffling noise on the stairs and the grunting of men lifting a heavy burden. Cara watched as an ornate pianoforte, under Evers' direction, was brought into the room and placed near the window.

Cara gasped as she recognized the instrument—a Broadwood—and she paled as she suddenly remembered the casual conversation with Garth. "I would prefer a Broadwood. Even Mister Beethoven…"

"Who is it from?" Aunt Lutie asked.

"We'll soon find out," said Evers, lifting off the envelope that had been stuck to the music rack, and handing it to Cara.

As she read the note, her face drained of color.

"What's the matter, Cara?" Aunt Lutie asked, seeing the tears well up in her eyes.

"It's…it's from Garth."

"Garth?" all three repeated.

"He must have ordered it before he sailed," Aunt Lutie speculated.

"Yes, that must be it," Cara said uncertainly.

"Well, it's a lovely present. And now I won't feel guilty about taking my own instrument back home with me."

Aunt Lutie always knew the right thing to say.

The day that Cara had heard the sad news of the shipwreck, she had closed the lid of Aunt Lutie's pianoforte and refused to play or sing. But she could not neglect this beautiful instrument; for it was a gift, to be used in remembrance…

Cara smiled and wiped her eyes. "Come, let's finish opening our presents, and then we'll sing carols. I'm eager to hear my lovely new pianoforte."

The opening of presents continued. When Cara exclaimed over the amethyst earrings that Calhoun had given her, he said, "They're to match your eyes."

"Aunt Lutie, do you think I should accept such an expensive gift from a man I hardly know?" Cara giggled.

"I expect this one time it will be all right."

Evers waited while Cara unwrapped his present to her. He watched as she peered into the little box at the exquisite miniature portrait. The pale yellow dress with the lilies-of-the-valley was hers, and the golden hair was pinned as she usually wore it.

"But how did you…?" Cara exclaimed.

Evers laughed. "Do you remember the short, bearded fellow who came to play chess with me?"

"Yes. He came four or five times, as I remember, and then I didn't see him again."

Evers smiled. "He was the artist. I told him that I wanted a miniature of you without your knowing it. While I took a long time to make my moves, he had the opportunity to study you.

"He's a mighty poor chess player, but a good artist." Evers lowered his voice. "I call it the 'Ginny Mia.' "

Cara laughed. "I love it, Brother-in-law."

"And I love your beautiful watercolor," Evers replied.

"We all love our paintings, Cara," Aunt Lutie interjected. "You're a talented young lady."

"*Perhaps you will paint one for me sometime.*" Garth's words came back to haunt her. She would gladly paint anything for her husband if she could only bring him back.

What a strong hold he had on her. She still saw everything through Garth's eyes and remembered almost every word that he had spoken to her. Was her life to be forever like this—bound to him in death as strongly as she had been in life?

"Cara, come back to us. You're a thousand leagues away."

She had not realized that Calhoun was watching her. "Have we finished opening the presents?" Cara asked. "Then, let's gather around and sing some of the carols. What will it be?"

"How about 'Bring a Torch, Jeannette Isabella'? I like that name," Evers commented. "If I ever have a wife, that's what I'm going to call her." He looked at Cara and smiled.

"Jeannette Isabella? You're as bad as Garth." Cara laughed. "Will the poor wife not have any say-so?"

"None, whatever."

"And you, Calhoun—do you have a special name for your future wife?"

"I rather prefer 'Ginny'," he drawled.

Evers glared at him, and Cara, anxious to avoid a confrontation, quickly began playing the carol.

They all sang loud and strong. An enthusiastic Aunt Lutie was slightly off-key, but it made no difference. The two men chose one carol after the other, but it was when they were arguing over the final one, that the slight movement of the china cupboard next to the fireplace caught Cara's eye.

She gave a little cry.

"What is it, Cara?" Evers asked.

"I...I thought I saw someone. Behind the cupboard."

"It's been a long evening and we're all tired. I think we should retire," Aunt Lutie suggested. She then turned to Calhoun. "Will you be staying the night, Cal?"

"No, Aunt Lutie. My town house is ready and waiting for me."

"Then, Evers, snuff out the candles on the tree," Aunt Lutie said. "We wouldn't want the house to burn down on Christmas Eve."

Chapter 27

*A*fter everyone else had gone to bed, Cara, unable to sleep, began to think of the sudden movement late that evening of the cupboard in the drawing room. Had she only imagined it? Or had there actually been someone watching them?

She knew that many of the earlier houses had been built with secret stairs, and even some with escape tunnels all the way to the river, but she had never knowingly been in such a house before.

Finally, she got up, lit a candle, and slipped into the drawing room. Kneeling down, she pressed against the lower panel of the cupboard, but it was solid. How stupid of her! It was the middle of the night. If anyone saw her like this, he would be sure that she had lost her mind.

Rising from the floor, she stepped on her long gown, causing her to stumble. When she pushed out her hand to right herself, the cupboard moved.

Suddenly fearful, Cara shuddered. It was far too

dark to explore further, but now she was certain. Her imagination had not gotten the better of her. There *was* a secret passage in the house, and someone had used it to spy on them that night.

Reluctantly, Cara slipped back to her bedroom. But she promised herself that as soon as the sun came up the next morning, she would continue the exploration.

The house was still quiet when Cara, fully dressed, made her way to the drawing room. Looking at the cupboard, so innocent looking with its porcelain plates and vases, to match the twin one on the other side of the hearth, she pressed; she touched; she felt all along the length and breadth of the fireplace and the mantel, but the spring to open the cupboard eluded her.

Yet, remembering her stumble the night before, she got down on her hands and knees to explore further.

"Did you lose somethin', Miss Cara?" Russell asked, walking into the room.

"One of my earrings," she answered quickly. "But I've found it."

Cara stood up and then made her way downstairs, adjusting the amethyst earring as if she were putting it back on.

Bells began to chime all over Charleston. It was Christmas Day, a joyous celebration, and Cara could not understand why such a miraculous event was ignored by so many sections of the country. But the celebration in the Stevens household continued.

By lunchtime, though, Calhoun had not reappeared,

Had he partied too much after leaving the Christmas Eve dinner? Finally, Aunt Lutie sent Henry to his town house to make sure he was awake, but her nephew was not there. He had simply vanished again.

He was fast becoming a puzzle to Aunt Lutie, with his various comings and goings, and not letting anyone know where he was going or where he had been.

Put out at his behavior, Aunt Lutie said, "Russell, go ahead and serve our meal. It seems that Mister Calhoun is not joining us today."

By mid-afternoon, with all conversation dying down like the fire on the hearth, Evers said, "How about some fresh air? It's a sunny day, so would my two best girls like to take a jaunt into the outside world?" He looked from Cara to Aunt Lutie, and back again. "It seems I have you both to myself today."

"You go ahead, Cara," Aunt Lutie suggested. "I have a terrible headache. I think I'll rest awhile, instead."

"I do hope you're not coming down with something, Aunt Lutie. Are you having chills, too?" Cara asked sympathetically, for the other woman was shaking slightly.

"No, it's those blasted bells. If they would only stop, I'd be fine."

"Would you rather I stayed with you?"

"Heavens, no! The fewer people in the house, the better...and the quieter it will be. Go on with Evers. It's not often that he's here in the middle of the day."

"Then I'll go and get my cloak," Cara responded,

eager to be outside.

Before she left, she went to the nursery to check on Carina. The baby had a small, raw scratch on her arm and she wanted to make sure that Molly had put some salve on it.

When she walked up the stairs to go into the nursery, she caught a brief glimpse of a black cloak and heard the sound of boots as a figure disappeared behind the door at the end of the hall.

Cara frowned. When she entered the nursery, she found only Molly, humming and rocking the baby to sleep.

"Molly, did someone come into the nursery?"

Molly looked up. "Sophie jes' finished nursin' the baby a minute ago, Miss Cara."

"But it wasn't Sophie I saw. Did a man come into the room?"

"No, ma'am," Molly replied, looking at Cara with a puzzled expression.

Unconvinced, Cara didn't pursue the subject. Instead, she said, "I wanted to make sure you put some more salve on Carina's arm. The scratch still looks a little raw."

"Yes'm, I'll do that, Miss Cara. I already trimmed her fingernails, so that should help."

When Cara met Evers downstairs, the two left the town house for their afternoon ride. Still thinking of the figure in the hall, she climbed into the carriage just as another carriage went rapidly past them.

The gasp coming from her throat caused Evers to

turn to her. "What is it, Cara?" he asked.

"Maida — It looked like Maida — the overseer's daughter from Mosshaven in that carriage."

"I doubt she would be in town today. Must have been somebody else."

"But what if it was Maida? On this street. And why did the one with her duck out of sight in such a hurry?"

Unbidden, unreasonable, the thought rushed through Cara's mind. Could it have been Garth? But that was impossible. Garth was dead.

Perhaps not! Who else would know of a secret passageway in the house? The man in the hall had possessed a long, familiar stride. And Elsine had said she'd seen him only a week after he was supposed to have sailed. And then, there was Margaret. She had questioned whether he had even gotten on the ship.

She didn't know why, but she had a feeling that she needed to return to the house. "Evers, I don't think the drive is such a good idea. Will you please take me back?"

"Are you not feeling well, Cara? Too much Christmas pudding, maybe?"

"Perhaps."

That night, the terror began. The scream came from the third floor nursery. Cara, not stopping to put on a robe or slippers, jumped from her bed and raced up the stairs to the nursery.

Molly was leaning over the cradle, sobbing.

"What is it, Molly? What has happened?" Cara

stared down at the empty cradle. "My baby! Where is my baby? Molly, where is Carina?"

"He took 'er, Miss Cara. I couldn't stop 'im."

"Who took her, Molly?" Cara's voice held all the anguish of a bereft mother.

"The man—the man in the dark cloak…"

Evers came running into the nursery. In the dim light of the candle, he looked at Cara, and then down at the empty cradle. His eyes were wide with disbelief.

"We have to stop him. He can't have my baby. I won't let him take my baby from me."

"Who, Cara? Who?"

"Garth. I saw him this afternoon in the house and he was the one in the carriage with Maida, I know. He's taken Carina away from me," she cried.

"Cara, get hold of yourself. Garth is dead. But even if, by some chance, he were still alive, he wouldn't kidnap his own child." Evers' voice was harsh.

"He would. He hates me. He promised to teach me a lesson I'd never forget."

"You're hysterical, Cara…Garth loved you…"

"Tell him, Molly. Tell him that Garth was here this afternoon."

"No, ma'am. Mister Garth never been heah, Miss Cara. That were a stranger that took 'er."

No one could console her, or convince her that it was not her husband who had stolen her child.

When Sheriff Hicks arrived, Evers explained, "She's had another shock, Sheriff, coming on top of her husband's death. She's not making sense. She has some far-fetched idea that Garth is alive and has kidnapped his own child."

Sheriff Hicks nodded in sympathy. "It's hard for her, I know, what with losing her memory, her husband, and now her baby. It's almost too much for one person to bear."

Cara sat, numb and unfeeling, hardly aware of the voices around her. When Sheriff Hicks put his hand on her shoulder, she lifted her eyes to his face. "Have faith, Mrs. Stevens. I'll do my best to find your child."

A search was made throughout Charleston and the surrounding countryside, but no trace of the baby could be found.

With Cara in such a state, someone was with her at all times. She felt imprisoned again, but this time by kindness and sympathy.

Regardless of what anyone said, Cara still believed that Garth had taken Carina, and consequently, everyone around her believed her to be mad. Only Cookie was the same towards her.

"I must get to him. I must make him understand. I'll do anything to get her back—anything."

Where would he have taken her? To Mosshaven, with Maida as his accomplice? Was she the one taking care of Carina? Or perhaps, Zellie? It wouldn't be so hard to bear if it were Zellie taking care of the golden-haired child and rocking her in the little cradle that she had brought down from the attic.

But Cara, determined to investigate on her own,

bided her time, on the surface acquiescing to leaving the search by the sheriff, while planning her next move.

It came sooner than expected, when several days later Evers said, "You're looking much better, Cara. I'm glad."

"Yes. I feel better, too. But I really would like to get out of the house, Evers. Do you…do you think you could take me for a drive this afternoon? And perhaps Cookie might like to go with me."

"Of course." Evers smiled at her.

Cara knew she must appear meek and manageable if her plan were to succeed. The last time she had tried to get the carriage herself, it had ended in defeat.

When the horses were hitched to the landau and brought to the side street, Cara, with her black cloak around her, climbed into the carriage with an excited Cookie seated opposite her.

"Oh, Evers, I forgot my sketchbook. It's in the sitting room. Would you mind getting it for me?"

The moment Evers disappeared into the house, Cara slapped the horses hard and made off as fast as the landau would travel.

"Why're we leavin' Mister Evers, Miss Cara?" a puzzled Cookie asked.

"It's a game, Cookie. Just wait and see." And she smiled at him in a conspiratorial manner.

"I love games," he answered. "Even iffen I don't understand 'em."

Cara hated playing a trick on Evers, but it was the only way she could leave the house unattended.

Although the carriage could not go nearly so fast as a rider on horseback, at least she had a headstart. It would take time for Evers to saddle a horse and follow her. And he would not know that she was going to Mosshaven.

They had almost reached the crossroads when she heard the horses. They would catch up with her too soon. She had no chance, unless—

Quickly Cara pulled into a clump of trees near the dense thicket. But if the riders glanced that way, they could not help but see the landau. And if one of them looked down at the road, he would be able to see the tracks leading into the trees.

"Hold the horses steady, Cookie, and try not to make any noise."

His eyes were big, but he did as Cara instructed.

She grabbed a dead pine branch and brushed away the telltale tracks only moments before the horses came into sight.

The riders went by in a gallop, the men neither slowing down nor looking to the right or left. But Evers was not in the group.

Realizing that the landau was a hindrance, Cara was convinced that it would be better to saddle one of the horses and leave the other one loose. But where could she get a saddle?

Had old Gregory taken Sonia's saddle when the horse returned from that first disastrous ride and put it back in the stable? The stable would be a good place to hide the landau, as well.

"Come, Cookie, let's get the carriage back on the road."

So instead of going to Mosshaven immediately, Cara headed toward Sonia's closed up plantation.

When they approached, a frowning Cara saw a curl of smoke ascending from one of the chimneys. Had Sonia leased her house to someone? But except for the smoke, the house looked deserted, and the grounds were in need of care.

"Where is we, Miss Cara?" Cookie asked in a loud voice.

"Ssh! Don't talk above a whisper. We're at a friend's house, but we must be very quiet."

Cara directed the horses past the house, and then circled back behind the row of necessaries at the far boundary.

"Wait here, Cookie, with the landau. I'm going to the stable to find a saddle."

A twig snapped under her foot and she stumbled. Picking herself up, she brushed off her cloak and continued on. She was ready to dart into the deserted building when angry voices reached her ears.

A woman was arguing with a man, and she sounded quite angry. That voice! Cara jumped back behind the stable.

Margaret McAlistair... What was she doing here? Then Cara saw the man. It was Frank Young, the man who had tried to take her from Mosshaven. What business did the Widow McAlistair have with Frank

Young? And why were they at Sonia's house?

"You are not to harm the baby, you understand?" the woman spoke in slow, angry tones.

"The brat's too much trouble, Maggie. It would be simpler—"

"I've told you I won't have it, and that's that!"

The baby? What baby? Were they talkng about Carina? Was her baby in Sonia's house? Oh, God! It was too much to hope for, but if it were true...

Frank Young went back into the house, and Margaret McAlistair rode out of the yard. Luckily, neither had seen her.

"Carina! Oh, Carina!" Cara whispered. Stealthily, she moved toward the house, looking into the dining room window, as she heard voices inside. Several men were seated at the table—eating, drinking, and joking among themselves. When one looked up, she jumped back out of sight.

"What is it, Frank?" one of the men asked.

"I thought I saw something move out there."

The other man laughed. "Garth Stevens is dead, even though Maggie isn't convinced. But you seem to jump every time something moves. Was it his ghost you saw, Frank?" the man teased. "You think he's coming back to haunt you for stealin' his brat?"

"Aw, cut it out!"

Cara was shivering from the cold. She knew that Cookie was probaby cold, too. But she had to wait and find out where they were keeping the baby.

Cara crept from one window to another. Then, she

saw her, in the alcove off the sitting room and she was nursing greedily. There was no mistake. It was Carina.

But how could she rescue her child? She could not possibly squeeze through the tiny, narrow window that was set high in the wall. Cookie was the only one small enough to climb in.

She left the protection of the overgrown shrubbery and swiftly made her way back to Cookie and the impatient horses.

"Did you get the saddle, Miss Cara?" Cookie asked.

Cara had completely forgotten about the saddle. "I've found Carina," she whispered. "We won't need the saddle. Will you help me rescue my baby, Cookie?" she pleaded.

"What'll I have to do?"

"Climb through a window and hand her to me. But you'll have to be very quiet. The bad men who kidnapped her are in the house."

Cookie's eyes widened.

Seeing his fright, she said, "You'll do this for me, won't you, Cookie? And everyone will know that you were the one to rescue her."

Cookie nodded, even though his eyes still indicated his fear.

Keeping the horses hitched to the landau, Cara took the reins and tied them to a tree branch. It was getting dark far too soon and Cookie, in his light coat, began to shiver.

"All right, Cookie. Let's go," she said, enfolding the little boy in her black cloak as they walked together.

By the time they reached the window, Cara saw that Carina had finished nursing. She waited until the woman had put the baby down and left the room. Then she began working on the window.

The latch was not firm in the fragile old wood and, with several tugs, she was able to loosen it. The window, long stuck, made a creaking noise as she pushed it open. Holding her breath, she waited to see if anyone would come to investigate the slight noise. But it went undetected.

Cara knelt down and whispered to Cookie, "Climb on my shoulders."

When Cookie was balanced and holding on to her forehead, an unsteady Cara finally stood up.

The boy climbed through the narrow window and sprang to the floor, heading to the drawer of the highboy that served as a makeshift bed for the baby. Carefully picking her up, he walked back to the window, but there he stopped.

The window was much too high for him to crawl out with the baby, or even hand Carina to Cara's waiting hands. Perplexed, he looked up at Cara.

"The chair, Cookie," she whispered frantically. "Use the chair."

His face brightened, but when he put the sleeping baby back into her bed, Carina stirred and whimpered.

"Please, Carina, don't cry. Please stay asleep," Cara prayed.

Cookie dragged the chair to the window and then went back for the baby. With all his strength, he climbed up on the chair and handed Carina to Cara's outstretched arms. Then, he scrambled out the narrow window and dropped to the ground.

Running breathlessly to the carriage, Cara, placing Carina in Cookie's arms, untied the reins. The horses snorted as the landau escaped. But they had made entirely too much noise. Someone would be sure to come after them.

She knew she would never be able to make it safely all the way back to the town house. There was only one place near enough to seek refuge. She must return to Mosshaven.

Chapter 28

The rider following them had nearly overtaken the landau. With Cookie holding the crying baby in his small arms, Cara urged the horses faster and faster.

"Cara," a voice shouted. "Slow down. You'll wreck the landau."

It was Evers.

Cara began to slow the carriage while Carina continued to cry.

By the time Evers pulled up beside her, a trembling Cara said, "Oh, Evers, I'm so thankful it's you."

"What foolishness made you go off without me?" He was beginning to sound like Garth.

"I had to find my baby, Evers, and we did — Cookie and I."

"Are you all right, and the baby — is she well?"

"I think so, only I'm so…exhausted."

"Stop the carriage. I'll tie my horse to the back and then I'll drive."

She obeyed him and, once again, she was sitting beside him. She waited for his rebuke at her deception. It was not long in coming.

"You're a headstrong little wench," he began.

Where had she heard those words before?

When they approached the long avenue of live oaks with its Spanish moss swaying in the breeze, the house was barely visible through the mist.

Cara realized that she was not the only one to return to Mosshaven with a feeling of trepidation. Evers had vowed that he would never return as long as Garth was alive. But Garth was dead. Evers had kept his vow.

Yet, when the house suddenly appeared through the icy mist, Cara felt nothing sinister about it. To her, it seemed a safe haven, welcoming her and her child.

With their arrival, Cara and Evers were surrounded by Zellie, James, and the other servants. The questions came rapidly, while Zellie took up Carina and snuggled her against her ample bosom.

"Little golden-haired baby—look jes' like your mama." Carina let out an angry wail. "And a temper jes' like your papa."

Cookie stood alone, his eyes blinking heavily. Cara leaned down and hugged him. "Somebody take care of Cookie. I think he must be quite hungry. He's the one who rescued Carina from those men. I couldn't have done it without Cookie."

"Emma," Zellie called, "feed this chile and put 'im to bed. He's done a good day's work for such a little man."

"I expect Carina will be hungry, too, within the next few hours. Is there anyone…?"

"I'll send for Vangie," Zellie said. "She's got more'n

enough milk for two."

"Poor Carina. She's been passed from one wet nurse to another. I hope she's not going to be upset."

"Milk is milk, Miss Cara. When you're hungry, it don't matter." Zellie laughed.

When Evers came downstairs, he had a pistol in his hand. "We can't be too careful. But what I don't understand is why anyone would kidnap Carina. Nevertheless, whatever the reason, we'll make sure no one does it again."

James locked all the doors and checked all the windows. And for the first time since Carina had been taken, Cara slept well, with her baby at her side.

The next day when they headed back to town, six armed riders rode in escort around the carriage that held Cara , the baby, Evers, and Cookie.

With the steady sway of the carriage, both Cookie and Carina fell asleep before they had reached the crossroads.

In a quiet voice, Cara turned to Evers and said, "I know you must be tired to be tied to a promise, Evers, and I... I'm tired of staying in town. Both you and Aunt Lutie have been wonderful and I'm so grateful. But I want to come back to Mosshaven. So, as soon as we get back safely, I'm releasing you from the burden of watching after me."

"Cara," he said slowly, "you must know that I'm in love with you..."

"Oh, Evers…"

"Don't interrupt, Cara," he begged. "It's hard enough to find the words without your frowning at me. When Garth asked me to take care of you, he didn't know that I would grow to love you and Carina as if you already belonged to me. I want to marry you and be a father to Carina—if…if you will have me."

"But I—"

"Don't say anything yet. I know it's too early to speak, but I couldn't wait any longer. Of course I realize that we can't marry until a year has passed. And that's why, if I'm to run the plantation, you can't come back to Mosshaven until after September. I will not have you a subject for gossip, Cara. You'll have to stay in town with Aunt Lutie to chaperone you.

"Naturally, I won't leave until this business of the kidnapping is cleared up. After that, I'll go to Mosshaven and come into town to see you every chance I get."

For Cara, there did not seem to be anything else she could say. Evers had planned her life for her. Today was not the day to tell him that Garth would always be between them.

In silence, Cara thought of the events of the past twenty-four hours. She had been so wrong about so many things—and she was now ashamed that she had suspected Garth, when it had been Frank Young all along. But Margaret McAlistair—she had never suspected her.

"What do you think will happen to Margaret Mc-

Alistair?" Cara asked.

"If the woman has any sense," Evers suggested, "she won't wait for Sheriff Hicks to arrest her. I expect she's already on her way to Barbados or some other hideaway."

Cara became reflective for the remainder of the ride back to town. Nothing made any sense to her. From the time that she had first come to Mosshaven, her life had been turned upside down.

When they returned, Louis Devereau was at the town house, calling on Aunt Lutie.

After the excitement had finally quieted down and the baby fussed over by the entire household, Louis turned to Aunt Lutie.

"I've really come to say good-bye, Lutie. I'm on my way back to Pendleton. I've left my plantation far too long. You may say no to me a thousand times, but I'll be back to press my suit after the cotton is planted."

Aunt Lutie blushed, but seemed pleased. Had she softened toward him? Cara believed she would eventually weaken and make Louis Devereau her fourth husband.

And then the thought struck her. Was she on her way to becoming another Aunt Lutie? Here she was— nineteen years old— and already a mother, a widow, and now proposed to by another man. But Cara was not eager to marry again. She had not even made a success of her first marriage.

That evening, Calhoun appeared again. He had disappeared so many times that no one was any longer surprised at his comings and goings.

"I hear there was a little excitement while I was gone," he said, joining the family for dinner.

"Wherever Cara is, it seems there's excitement," Evers commented. "But after we're married—"

"What?" Calhoun interrupted. "What do you mean?" His face was livid.

"Please don't...don't talk like this. I've made no promises..." Cara looked pleadingly from Evers to Calhoun, and Aunt Lutie stared at them all in stunned amazement.

"You are no gentleman, Evers, speaking like this. You've not only insulted Cara, but also your dead brother's honor."

"I've insulted no one, Cal. You're just angry because you covet her, as well."

"Evers! Cal!" Aunt Lutie admonished. "Think of Cara. Don't fight over her before her very eyes!"

"I agree, Aunt Lutie. Hanging Oak is a better place to resolve this matter," Cal responded.

"Are you challenging me, Cal?"

His cousin nodded.

"Well then, by God, I'll take you up on it," Evers replied. "Tomorrow at sunrise?"

Calhoun smiled as he asked, "What is your choice of weapons?"

"No!" Cara cried. "You're both too dear to me. I won't have it."

The two men ignored her.

"Pistols at twenty paces," answered Evers in response to Calhoun's question.

"Then sunup it is." Calhoun slapped his napkin on the table and left the house.

"Evers, please. I beg of you…Don't meet him. Don't go through with this awful thing," Cara pleaded, laying her hand on his sleeve.

"It's too late, Cara. My honor is at stake. Would you prefer a coward for a husband?"

His mind was made up, and there was nothing that either Cara or Aunt Lutie could say to dissuade him. Not finishing dinner, Evers left the house to make provisions for the hastily arranged duel.

The celebration of rescuing Carina had disintegrated, replaced by the knowledge of what was to occur on the next day.

Cara felt guilty. What could she do to stop this madness? How would she ever be able to live with herself, knowing she was the cause of this terrible breach in Garth's family?

That night, she stayed awake for hours, trying to come up with a solution, but there seemed to be no answer, unless…

Early the next morning, Cara, determined to stop the duel, at any cost, listened for Evers to leave the house and then she ran to the carriage house.

Henry protested as she ordered him to hitch the horses to the landau. But she was the mistress , so he obeyed her.

As the carriage wheels sank into the ruts of the road

leading to Hanging Oak, Cara prayed that the two hotheaded men would also obey her before it was too late.

Recklessly, she drove the landau, silently apologizing to the horses as she sped along the sandy road.

All around her, the mist was thick, hanging close to the ground. But even in the mist, Cara could feel the uneasiness of the land as she approached Hanging Oak—that ancient sentinel of bygone days when justice was immediate and the doubts came later.

Shivering in the cold, gray mist, with only a tinge of yellow on the horizon, Cara suddenly came to a stop.

If only she could see…

Almost in answer to her wish, the sun knifed through the mist. And that was when she saw them—their backs to each other; each taking measured steps until the disembodied second called them to halt.

Without bothering to tie the reins, Cara jumped to the ground. She ran past the oak , hurrying to get between them in time. But it was already too late.

A few seconds after the order of "Fire!" was issued from unknown lips, Cara felt a sudden burning in her shoulder. She spun from the blow while briefly watching two men running toward her before she fell, face forward.

A few minutes later, Calhoun, pressing his handkerchief on her wound, said, "It's only a glance.The bullet didn't go in."

"Thank God!" Evers' voice held great relief. "I would

never have forgiven myself if..."

"Promise me — " Cara whispered.

"Anything," Evers said, his face pale with anxiety.

"Promise me...you will be friends again."

The landau had disappeared, the horses spooked by the sound of pistols. So side by side, two saddle horses gingerly made their way home. One carried an extra load; for Calhoun held Cara in his arms, while Evers, silent and moroseful, kept a close watch on the pale, still figure wrapped in her black cloak.

On the way, they found the landau and the horses by the side of the road, so Cara was transferred to the carriage. But this time, it was Evers who took over, driving the carriage, as he had done several days previously.

When they arrived, a nervous Aunt Lutie was waiting in the entrance hall.

Even though her cloak parted to reveal the bloodied handkerchief and the torn part of her dress, Cara assured the woman that she was all right.

"What is this? A new form of dueling?" Aunt Lutie's voice cried. "Whose bullet hit her?"

"In truth, we don't know," Evers answered. "It's her left shoulder, but she whirled first one way and then another."

"I suppose that is your just reward for such an idiotic action. Now you'll both share the guilt although you can't share the girl."

"But they'll share being alive, Aunt Lutie," Cara said "And for that, I'm quite thankful."

Chapter 29

*D*uring the next weeks, as Cara's shoulder healed, the uneasy truce between Calhoun and Evers remained.

Although she tried to make Calhoun feel welcome, he seldom came to visit and that, only when Evers was away. Then he disappeared entirely, as he was wont to do in the past.

Evers was also away much of the time, seeing that the new crops of cotton were planted, and the rice fields looked after at Mosshaven. The young man, so irresponsible in the past, had grown up, taking a man's place with a man's responsibilities.

And as for Margaret McAlistair, it was as Evers had predicted—she had disappeared, with only the overseer in charge.

It had now been well over a year since Cara had come to the Low Country, and she was still no closer to solving the mystery of her brother Bart's death. Neither had she solved the mystery of the secret passageway next to the fireplace.

One day while sitting in the drawing room, Cara turned to her husband's relative. "Aunt Lutie, did Garth ever mention a secret stairway to you?"

"Here? In this house?"

Cara nodded.

"No, Cara—but it's possible—a secret passage. Why do you ask?"

Cara hesitated. "Do you remember on Christmas Eve when I was upset because I thought I saw someone staring at me?"

"You were only tired, and your imagination—"

"No," she interrupted. "I saw the china cupboard move and there was a man behind it."

"Are you sure, Cara?" Aunt Lutie looked at her in alarm.

"Yes. I didn't tell anyone, but that night after you were all asleep, I slipped out of bed to check. I stumbled and fell against something—the mechanism, I suppose—and the cupboard actually moved. But in the dark, I was too frightened to investigate further, so I went back to bed.

"Early the next morning, before breakfast, I returned to the drawing room. I pushed; I prodded; I felt all along the side of the mantel, but I couldn't find it again."

"Why have you waited so long to confide in me, Cara? Why didn't you say something to me when it happened?" Aunt Lutie asked.

"I was afraid you might think I had lost my mind and was seeing ghosts."

Aunt Lutie leaned forward. "Ghosts? Whom did you think you saw, Cara?"

"That night, I thought it was Garth."

Aunt Lutie's eyes widened in surprise. "And is that why you got the idea that it was Garth who had kidnapped little Carina?"

"Yes," an embarrassed Cara admitted.

Aunt Lutie appeared to be thinking hard. Finally, she spoke. "If what you say is true, and there really is a secret passage, then we are all in danger from someone using that staircase. The only thing for us to do is find it, if it exists."

Aunt Lutie made her way to the china cupboard. She felt from one shelf to another while Cara watched.

"I remember a ghost story I heard as a girl—about an old house on Edisto Island," Aunt Lutie began. "It also had a secret passageway. Somehow a group of smugglers found it and was using it to get from the sheltered cove where they brought their goods in by boat."

Aunt Lutie stopped her story as she struggled to get down on her knees to search lower. And then she continued.

"There was a deaf old lady who lived all alone in that house, except for one servant. One night, the smugglers made so much noise that even *she* heard them. But there was a tragic end to the story.

"The old lady was so frightened that she had the wall bricked up. Several nights later, a group of hostile Indians came and attacked her. She was found the next day in front of the brick wall, with her hands bloody from trying to remove the bricks from the passageway.

"For years, on the anniversary of her death, that same noise could be heard—hands scratching upon brick—and there were always fresh drops of blood on the floor."

"Do you really believe that story, Aunt Lutie? It sounds like something to frighten little children on Hallow's Eve."

"Well, whether it's true or not, we should let that be a lesson to us. I don't mean we'll have to run from marauding Indians, but it would be safer if a passageway *is* found, to make sure we could use it to get out, but no one could get in."

"Perhaps if we find it, maybe we could remove the spring mechanism from the other side," Cara suggested.

Pushing herself up from the floor, Aunt Lutie's face was flushed, whether from excitement or exertion, Cara could not tell.

"Well, the spring has to be *somewhere*. How did you get it to open that night?"

"I don't really know. It moved when I fell, so it must be low."

"Did you put your hand out to catch yourself?"

Cara thought for a moment. "Yes, I believe I did."

"Then why don't *you* try it again, and let's see what happens."

Cara felt foolish as she crouched, but she closed her

eyes, trying to recall her position that dark night. At the same time, she hoped that Russell would not appear unexpectedly and find her repeating her action as he had that previous morning. She could not use the lost earring story again.

Trying to remember the sequence of that earlier night, Cara closed her eyes and began the slow, methodical reenactment of her former actions.

She felt along the cupboard, gradually moving her hands downward, until she reached the small triangular onyx decoration bordering the side of the fireplace. Slowly, the cupboard shifted.

"It's moving," Aunt Lutie whispered, excited at Cara's success.

Together, the two women pushed the small opening wider to peer into the stairwell.

"Do you think this is how the intruder got in to kidnap Carina?" Cara asked.

"More than likely," Aunt Lutie replied.

"Do we dare…?"

Aunt Lutie shivered. "No, Cara. Let's leave it alone for now, and wait for Evers."

Cara agreed.

Aunt Lutie could hardly wait for Evers to arrive and show him what she and Cara had discovered.

Once Aunt Lutie broached the subject, a surprised Evers said, "No, Garth never mentioned this to me, Aunt Lutie. And since the house is old, he may not even have known about a secret passage when he bought it. But then if it were well known, there wouldn't have been any use for it."

"Do you think, Evers, that you can fix it so no one can get in from the other side?" Cara asked.

"Probably, but we'll have to be careful. Russell can be trusted, I'm sure, to help and keep the secret. Who knows, one day we might have need of it." He thought for a moment before adding, "We must make sure, though, that it leads somewhere. I wouldn't want to be trapped in that dark hole."

Cara and Aunt Lutie both shuddered at the thought.

With Russell's help, after Evers determined, despite the spiderwebs and a few bugs, that the passageway led to safety, the inside spring was removed and the cupboard pushed back into place.

Cara now felt safe from any intruders, and life continued on as usual, until a week had passed.

On that next Wednesday morning, Cara awoke to a strange, gray day. She became aware of a thickness in the air, a pungent odor, much like seared, scorched material dipped in water, that irritated her throat.

Evers and Aunt Lutie, noticing it too, sat uneasily at the breakfast table, as Cara joined them. Before the three had finished with breakfast, the bells over town began to ring with a slow and mournful clang.

"Russell," Evers said, "go out into the street and see if you can discover what's happening."

A few minutes later, when he returned, he said, "There's a fire, Mr. Evers. Down at the docks — but that's all I found out. Don't know how bad it is."

Evers stood up. "I'd better go, then. The fire volunteers will need all the help they can muster."

"Will you send word to us, Evers—if there's a danger in its coming this way?"

"I'll take Henry with me, Cara. He can bring the message back with him."

To Cara and Aunt Lutie, the waiting seemed interminable. They were both aware of how fast a fire could spread from one wooden building to another, especially when the wind was strong.

An hour later, when Henry returned, Aunt Lutie immediately asked, "Is it bad, Henry? Did Evers say we needed to get ready to leave?"

"No'm. It ain't that bad. Mister Evers say jes' to stay put until he gets back. He don't think there's any danger to the town yet."

Late in the afternoon, when Evers returned to the town house, he was tired and smokestained from the long hours of fighting the fire. "I think we have the fire contained," he said. "We've put up barricades, so unless the wind shifts, we're safe."

The odor lingered in the air all night , and by the next morning it still had not vanished, although the wind was still.

Again, Evers went to the dock area.

By the second afternoon, having no word from Evers, who had remained at the dock, Aunt Lutie became anxious about her own house.

"It would just be like my servants to get scared and leave my house open for any thief or scavenger who might be lurking. I think I'd better go and put some backbone in Jasper. I won't be long, Cara."

"That's a good idea, Aunt Lutie. But please be careful when you're out on the street."

Soon after Lutie left in the carriage driven by Henry, Cara became aware of a haze, now drifting like a lazy, spreading cloud, and silently making its approach up the street.

The silence suddenly became disrupted by rumbles of thunder in the distance, and the wind marred the uneasy truce as it began to rise, growing and unleashing its power.

At the height of the fury, a worried Evers returned.

"The wind has shifted, Cara. New fires are spreading and the dense smoke is pouring out into our direction. You're not safe here, so we'll need to leave for Mosshaven at once."

"But Aunt Lutie isn't here," Cara informed him. "We can't leave until she gets back."

"Where did she go?"

"To check on her own house."

"And she took one of the carriages?"

"Yes—the landau. And Henry drove her."

"Russell," he shouted, "get the other carriages out and see that all the servants are gathered together."

"Will we be able to pack anything?"

"No, Cara. There's little time left and besides, there's not enough room—hardly enough to hold everyone."

Seeing her disappointment, he added, "…just the necessities…but nothing large or heavy."

Did he know that she was thinking of the portrait?

All the servants quickly gathered and Evers divided them into groups, assigning them places in the carriages. Russell would take one of the larger carriages; Henry would take the other, and Evers would drive the landau with Aunt Lutie, Cara, and the baby Carina.

Impatient for Aunt Lutie and Henry to return, Evers paced up and down. "Russell, I think you'd better go on with your group. Don't wait for us. I'll have to go after my aunt if she doesn't return soon."

"How much time do we have, Evers?" Cara asked.

"When I left an hour ago, the fire was already getting close to the main road."

Hearing the front door open and close, a relieved Cara said, "That must be Aunt Lutie now."

"I really didn't need such a bright welcome to find my way home."

"Calhoun," Cara exclaimed. "We thought you were Aunt Lutie."

Calhoun, devastatingly handsome in a new riding habit and cloak, stood in the hallway.

"Is Aunt Lutie not here?"

"She's at her house, and she took the landau with her," Cara answered.

"Cal, did you come in your phaeton?" Evers asked.

"No. I'm on horseback." He saw the worried look. "Is the fire that dangerous? I'll go after Aunt Lutie, if you need me to do so."

Cara turned to Evers. "Please don't wait any longer. Take the baby, with Molly and Sophie, and I'll wait for Calhoun to return with Aunt Lutie and Henry. I can ride in the landau with them."

"No, Cara. I won't leave you here alone."

"Not even for Carina? Please, Evers..." Her voice was soft and pleading.

"I'll take good care of Cara, " Calhoun promised. "I'll be back with Aunt Lutie and the landau before you've been gone five minutes—and I promise to pass you on the road, Cousin."

Evers still hesitated, but Cara insisted. "Please, Evers...if you love me..."

Molly brought Carina into the sitting room. Cara wrapped the sleeping baby in her blanket, kissed the little cherub face, and handed her back to Molly.

"Hurry, Evers, I'll be all right." Cara smiled to reassure him.

The horses, catching the scent of danger in the air, began whinnying and pawing the ground. Evers gave Cara one last, loving look and then he was gone.

Cara walked back into the house alone. There was nothing left for her to do except to wait for Calhoun's return.

The moments ticked away. The faint, distant noises of a city choking in smoke were all that Cara could hear. No sound of horses in the street... no sound of people coming or going... She suddenly felt as if she were the only person left in the universe.

A lonely, chilling feeling crept over her, as heavy as her black winter cloak. She climbed the stairs to the drawing room to take one last look at the *Cara Mia*, which she would be leaving behind.

Despite her initial dislike, she knew that she was irrevocably linked to the portrait. As she examined it, she realized that it was here that she felt the strongest link to her husband. It seemed that all of her pain, and yes— all her joy—had stemmed from his love of the painting.

She rose from the sofa and stood before it, seeing it in a new light. Had she changed, or had the portrait the power to both soothe and challenge her?

But what was it that had disturbed her so about the portrait? Walking closer, she began to examine each minute stroke of the artist's brush, her eyes looking beyond the face to the barely visible tapestry in the far corner of the painting.

Subtly embroidered in the faded tapestry was an element she had never noticed before—the heraldic arms, with an ornate dagger in the center.

The shock caused her to shiver. Was it not similar to the ones that had sought to do her harm so recently? Why had she not noticed it before? Was it because she had never taken the time to examine the painting this closely?

The puzzle only added to her dismay. Suddenly, she did not want to leave the painting behind. There was something about it that called to her, begging her to remember…

When she heard the sound of footsteps up the stairs, Cara was relieved. Calhoun had returned and she could now leave.

"Calhoun," she called, "I'm in the drawing room. Do you think there'll be room to take the painting with us? I would hate for it to be damaged by the smoke."

When he didn't answer, she turned to the doorway.

"Well, Ginny—looks like you're by yourself. What bad luck for you."

Chapter 30

"*W*hat are you doing here?" Cara demanded. "How dare you invade my house! My cousin is returning any moment, and he'll certainly deal with you!"

Frank Young laughed. "Is that so?" he said as he walked toward her.

Cara backed away. "What do you want?"

"It's not what *I* want," he replied. "It's what the Blades of Acheron have demanded."

It was then that she saw the knife in his hand. Her eyes widened in recognition. "Why?" she asked, her voice barely above a whisper.

"Because your brother betrayed us, Ginny Carter. I'm only dealing out the last measure of justice."

He grabbed her, but Cara struggled loose and ran behind the massive pianoforte near the window. Watching him coming closer, with the wicked knife in his hand, she asked, "Was he…was he one of you?"

"Yes, for a while. But he had no stomach for it."

"But why are you punishing me?" Cara asked. If she could only keep him engaged in conversation long enough for Calhoun to return, she would have a chance.

"It's the justice in the Articles of Agreement. A man thinks twice when he knows his entire family will be wiped out if he betrays the cause."

"What cause?"

Seeing the fright on her face, Frank Young seemed to be enjoying the cat and mouse game. He made no effort to advance farther, but watched her with pleased, beady eyes.

"Privateering — or pirating, if you want to call it that. We waited for the ships leaving Charleston, loaded with cotton and rice. Your husband had the best, and we considered it a fine prize when we were able to capture one of his cargoes. Too bad he didn't let you go with me that day I came for you. Maybe he would be alive today."

A sense of horror swept over her. "You...you sank the *Northrop*?"

He chuckled appreciatively at her quick perception.

In the overwhelming anger that this man had deliberately killed her husband, she forgot her own danger. Without thinking, she rushed from the safety of the massive Broadwood pianoforte and turned on him like a vixen.

With no weapon except her own body, she attacked him, kicking and scratching him until the blood streamed from the contact of her fingernails to his face.

Uttering an oath, he grabbed her, jerking her arms behind her.

"I had intended killing you quickly, but I think a slow, painful death will pleasure me more."

"Like the one you planned for me when you slashed the picture?" She was only guessing that he had been the culprit.

"That didn't work. I thought it was you in the picture."

He twisted her arm and, with rough, painful movements, he dragged her to the window, where he jerked down the tasseled ropes that held back the draperies.

"Appropriate, don't you think? Your husband's gift to you will keep you from escaping, while you slowly burn to death."

Playing for time, she asked, "And how did you know that the piano was a gift from Garth?"

He didn't answer her question. Instead, he proceeded to push her into the gilt chair before the pianoforte and tied her, binding her arms with one of the tasseled ropes. Using the other, he lashed the chair to the leg of the massive, ornate instrument.

Why did Calhoun not come? What was delaying him? If he didn't come soon, it would be too late.

"Help! Somebody help me," she screamed.

"You're very much alone, my beauty. There's no one within miles to hear you. A pity…someone as beautiful as you should not go to her death unlamented." He leaned over and pressed his warm, moist lips on hers, and she shuddered with revulsion.

Convinced that she was unable to free herself, he

lowered the chandelier from the ceiling and she watched as he lit each candle. And then, with one swift stroke of the knife, the chandelier fell down with a crash, the burning candles starting tallow-scented wisps of fire on the Aubusson rug.

Not content with the slow burning of the rug, he moved about the room, setting fire to the draperies.

"We must make sure that the stairs are on fire, too, in case someone tries to rescue you, when your beautiful face is being scorched by flames."

He took up the delicate wooden chairs, one by one, and broke them into firewood. Gathering the pieces of wood, Frank Young, with one last comment, disappeared from the drawing room.

As she struggled to get free, the dense smoke began to permeate the room. Cara coughed as the flames increased, leaping higher and higher, spreading across the walls to the ceiling. And then her head became light and she felt too tired to cough or even breathe. Vaguely she remembered thinking, Is this the way it feels to die?

As she gasped for air, Cara heard a noise downstairs, a sound of men's voices and furious blows. Had Calhoun finally come? But already, it was too late. He would never make it up the burning stairs, even if he got past Frank Young.

"Cara," the voice shouted. "Where are you?"

Struggling for breath, she lifted her head. "Upstairs—in the drawing room."

"Keep talking until I find you. I can't see!"

Strange, how one's mind, when deprived of oxygen,

plays tricks. She could have sworn that it was Garth, and not Calhoun who was calling out to her.

The man was coughing in paroxyisms as his voice came nearer. "I'm…I'm in the room. Where are you?"

"Tied to the pianoforte—by the window."

His hands groped for her and when he found her, he untied the rope that bound her and Cara was finally freed from the gilt chair.

"Cara Mia!" he managed to say.

"Oh, Garth," she cried. He was alive, after all. But had he come back, only to die trying to save her? Was this to be the end of their lives together, with no future and no hope of ever seeing their little daughter again?

The two struggled to reach the fireplace, just as part of the ceiling fell in.

"The painting, Garth. We have to save the painting."

"There's no time."

Cara choked. She felt as if her lungs were bursting.

Garth pushed open the cupboard and the sudden rush of cold air from the passageway was intoxicating. Cara's lungs drank in the air until the passageway, too, began to fill with smoke. Together they hurried down the steep steps, until Cara felt the dirt along the tunnel floor.

Garth groped along the wall, urging Cara with him. The dank odor of mold and mildew replaced the acrid odor of smoke.

Coughing again, a hoarse Cara asked, "Where does this tunnel lead?"

"To the cellar in a house on Tradd Street—where the

royal govenor once lived. It was built so he could escape capture at a moment's notice."

"Did you — did you use this tunnel before?" Cara inquired.

"Only once, on Christmas Eve."

With unsteady steps, Cara continued the journey. Just when she thought she might drop from exhaustion, they came to the end of the passageway — to the closed door.

"I hope that whoever is living in this house now, has already gone; for I'll have to break the door down," Garth admitted.

He strained against the door, but it did not budge. What if they were trapped? It would be too cruel for them to have gotten this far in their escape, only to be entombed in this dark tunnel. The Blades of Acheron would have won after all.

But then, Cara remembered another door that had been locked against him, and she knew that this door would be no match against her husband's great strength. True to her confidence in him, he wrested the door from its moorings, and they finally stepped into the cellar .

But they were not alone.

"So you came back to save her," the voice greeted him.

"Calhoun," Cara croaked in her smoke-damaged throat.

"It's too bad you didn't go down with the *Northrop*, Garth," Calhoun said as he pointed his pistol at the unarmed man.

"Calhoun, the leader. The last of the Blades of Acheron," Garth mocked.

"Yes. It's now down to just you and me. You may have destroyed everything, but the price has been high—paid with your life and Cara's."

"Let Cara go, Calhoun. She has done nothing to harm you."

"Are you begging, Cousin? I don't see you down on your knees."

"My knee does not bend to a common pirate. But my heart asks that you have some measure of decency as the sworn protector of a defenseless girl."

"A common pirate, as you call me, does not honor any vow to you. It ended when you turned to destroy me. Still, you may not believe it, but even after I found out she was Bart's sister and marked for death, I actually protected her for a while."

Calhoun looked at Cara with greedy eyes. "I desired her from the first time I saw her and thought to make her my wife after you were dead.

"But I found that my hate for you, Garth, was even stronger than my passion for Cara. I want to see you in agony. And what better way to accomplish this than to kill her before your very eyes? Death will seem sweeter to you, will it not, Cousin—after your beloved Cara is dead?"

He raised the pistol and as he aimed it at her, Garth spoke calmly. "Get behind me, Cara. Move quickly."

Cara was frantic. How could her husband hope to

defend both of them against Calhoun without a weapon?

Looking around, her eyes latched onto the iron tongs in the corner. She moved quickly, but not behind her husband.

Sensing the more immediate danger of the advancing man, Calhoun turned his attention to Garth.

When Calhoun cocked the pistol, Garth lunged, leaving a clear path as Cara, out of the line of fire, hurled the tongs in Calhoun's direction.

The tongs made direct contact with Calhoun's head, causing him to reel and stumble as the pistol fired.

Not knowing which man had been shot, Cara rushed to her husband's side. "Are you hurt?"

He stared at her and, with an ironic smile, said, "And who is she... terrible as an army with banners?"

Cara and Garth stared at the still body of Calhoun Wilkes, while blood began to stain the floor beneath him. Stunned by the tongs, he had fallen victim to his own pistol.

"Do you think he's dead?" a shaken Cara asked.

"He appears to be," Garth replied, sheltering Cara's face from Calhoun's body. And then, taking her hand in his, he said, "Come, cara mia, the pilot boat is waiting to take us upriver."

As they edged their way through the deserted streets, the sky was bright with the glow of burning houses.

Cara knew she shouldn't look back, but the urge

was overwhelming. The entire block where the town house stood was a bonfire. She felt a great sadness, grieving for the lost portrait, yet at the same time, feeling a sense of freedom with its destruction.

When they finally approached the dock, the pilot said, "I'd almost given up hope, Mister Stevens. I decided you weren't coming."

"It took a little longer than I anticipated," Garth replied.

Chapter 31

*O*n the way upriver, Garth tenderly wiped the soot from Cara's face. The two no longer resembled an elegant couple; for their clothes reeked of smoke. But that was of little import. They had found each other again. And that was all that mattered.

Exhausted, Cara leaned her head against her husband's shoulder.

"I'm so confused, Garth. So many questions…"

"I know, my love. It hasn't been an easy time for you. And it was hell for me to see you from a distance and not rush to take you in my arms and comfort you."

"But why did you pretend to leave on the *Northrop*, yet not let me know you were safe when it sank?"

"If we were to have a future together, I had to find out who was trying to kill you, Cara. And because I suspected everyone, it had to remain a secret. And women can not usually keep a secret," he added in a teasing manner.

She ignored the teasing. "Then, how did you find

out about Calhoun?"

"I had no idea, at first, that he could be involved. It was Sheriff Hicks and Maida who supplied the information about Bart and Calhoun's fight.

"He never bothered to soil his hands with the everyday affairs. Instead, he left all the dirty work to his henchman, Frank Young.

"Calhoun made just one mistake—your brother Bart. His temper got the better of him, and that was the beginning of his downfall."

"Do you mean it was Calhoun who killed my brother?"

"Yes."

"And the IOU…?"

"…Belonged originally to Evers. Bart pulled a knife on him in a fight over the gambling debt. I forced Evers to sell the IOU to me and I took the knife—that peculiar symbol of the Blades of Acheron—so there would be no bloodshed. Only I had not reckoned with Calhoun."

"But why did they kidnap Carina?" a still puzzled Cara asked.

"When their privateering venture was being destroyed, they suspected I might still be alive. They knew that the kidnapping would bring me out into the open. But you ruined their chances when you stole her back—under their noses, I might add."

Cara pulled away from Garth's embrace. "You just said that women can not keep secrets; yet Maida evidently did."

"She felt so guilty about putting the snake in your

armoire, that she would have done anything to make up for it... She was quite jealous of you at first, you know."

Cara nodded and, thinking again of Mosshaven, she began to put her thoughts into words.

"I...I hope that everyone has gotten safely to Mosshaven—including Aunt Lutie. Evers took the baby with him." She looked up at her husband and said, "Our daughter—you have seen her?"

"Yes. I couldn't stay away. I had to see her just once. She's beautiful—the image of her mother."

A rueful Cara smiled. "She may not like resembling someone else—just as I, at first, didn't like the idea of resembling your painting."

"You have it backwards, my love. The painting only reminded me of you."

"But how could that be? You bought the painting long before you ever saw me."

"That's not true. I was dazzled by your beauty when I first saw you in the gardens at Middleton, but then you disappeared. I nearly tore down Charleston and the entire countryside trying to find you. It was only later, when I had despaired of ever seeing you again, that I went to Europe—and found the painting."

"Then, you really loved me when you forced me to marry you?"

Garth's arms tightened around her. "I told you in a thousand ways. I even gave up being at the birth of my daughter—the comforts of home—so that I could destroy the danger that threatened you."

His voice softened. "But never fear, madam. I expect you to make it up to me when we get home."

The family reunion was a tired but joyful one. Zellie and Flora made it a celebration with a specially prepared dinner. And afterwards, as they gathered briefly, not in the drawing room, but in the comfortable library, Evers looked up at the empty space over the mantel, where the *Cara Mia* had once hung.

"It looks as if this room has need of another painting, " he said.

"What was there, first, before the *Cara Mia*?" Cara asked.

"Did Garth not tell you?" Evers replied. "It was a painting of the two of us as boys. But after our fight, Garth took it down."

He turned to Garth. "What did you do with it, Brother?"

"It's in the attic."

"Then, maybe you'll give it to me. I'll have need of a few furnishings of my own when I buy Margaret McAlistair's confiscated plantation."

Aunt Lutie joined in. "I can't believe that nice Widow McAlistair consorted with pirates!"

"Actually, she was a fence for the stolen cotton and rice," Garth said. "No one questioned her. The factors at the Exchange merely thought that her plantation was extremely successful."

* * *

That night, as Cara went to sleep, the strange dream, that had plagued her previously, reappeared.

Once again, she was in the old palazzo, sitting for her portrait. The chair, the tapestry, the familiar dagger... all were there. But the air was oppressive, filled with mystery and court intrigue.

The uneasiness in the streets gradually grew louder, until a dreaded knock at the entrance of the palazzo announced her would-be assassins—hired by her uncle, determined to wrest her inheritance from her.

Her husband drew his sword, but, despite his furious fighting, there were too many for one man, one sword, to overcome.

As she was dragged from the room, she heard the anguished cry of her grievously wounded husband.

"I will find you again, Cara Mia, even if I have to search to the ends of the earth!"

Cara awoke with tears in her eyes. The dream had vanished. She was no longer in the palazzo, but in Garth's arms, safe at last.

The mist from the river began its morning journey, enveloping the sentinel oaks, with the moss swaying in the gentle breeze.

From the nursery, she heard the cry of a hungry baby, demanding to be fed, while Mosshaven came alive.

She had come full circle, a momentous journey that

had spanned love, loss, and renewal through the centuries.

But all these things Cara Stevens was destined to keep locked in her heart.

§

About the Author

Frances Patton Statham has combined two careers and two loves—music and writing. She graduated *magna cum laude* from Winthrop University with a double major in voice performance and music education, holds a Master of Fine Arts degree from the University of Georgia, and an honorary doctorate from World University, with further opera study.

Whether sailing the Danube or the Rhine, exploring World War I trenches in France, or giving a voice recital in Budapest or Madrid, she has always been attuned to the next story to share with her readers.

A recipient of numerous awards in fiction, music composition, art, and community service, Statham lives in metro-Atlanta, Georgia.

Acknowledgments

Bright Sun, Dark Moon is a reprint of my first novel. It was accepted for publication by the first publisher to whom I sent the unsolicited manuscript—Ace Books.

At the time, I was a volunteer in a national organization and had been given the task of writing a safety program for our ninety thousand members to launch in their communities.

I had always been a storyteller, but with a music and drama background, I was more attuned to words sung, rather than words written in another form. So to gain a little expertise in a different style, I decided to take a nonfiction evening course at a local university. However, it was the same night as choir rehearsal, and as a soloist, I could not miss rehearsal. So I enrolled in a fiction class on another night, instead.

Although I missed four out of the eight sessions since I was conducting safety workshops in various states, those few sessions were enough to light the creative fire.

I shall always be grateful to Ace Books and also to the road block that led me to the fiction class and the beginning of an enjoyable writing career.

Frances Patton Statham

www.ingramcontent.com/pod-product-compliance
Lightning Source LLC
Chambersburg PA
CBHW070103260626
47160CB00004B/1301